PHANTOM'S
THRALL

JESSAMINE RUE

First Edition: May 2022

Rue, Jessamine
Phantom's Thrall / by Jessamine Rue—First edition.

1

1

BEFORE YOU BEGIN...

TRIGGER WARNINGS

Bondage, knife play, murder, stalking, threat of rape, dark elements, moments of dubious consent

AUTHOR NOTE

This book is loosely based on the novel "The Phantom of the Opera," by Gaston Leroux. Since the original novel is now in the public domain, it is legal to use names and plot elements in retellings.

This book contains detailed sex scenes (MMM+F) involving one or more partners of various genders.

CHRISTINE

My first sight of the soaring Lajeunesse Opera House sends a ripple of tingling delight over my skin. But I try not to show my reaction. I endeavor to keep my face placid and smooth, as Madame Theriault taught me.

All my life I've been told that I show my feelings too freely. I must conceal them under a pleasant calm unless I'm on the stage, when I may show only the emotions being displayed in the scene. Sometimes I fear that everything I'm concealing will spin out of my control and explode in a tempest of passion. And then I will be ruined, because girls in my situation are not allowed to want too much, or ask for too much.

I have lived all my life at the Marchette School for Young Ladies, where I was taken after the death of my father, Gustave Daaé. A famous violinist, he left behind just enough money for my care until I reached the age of eighteen, after which I stayed on at the school for another year, to assist with the younger students.

I would have stayed longer, but Madame Theriault said it was time for the bird to leave the nest, and that if I would not fly, she must give me a little shove. The Lajeunesse Opera House is asking for fresh young dancers, and I am one of the most talented girls at the Marchette School. Our most gifted girl is Elise, but she refused to take the opportunity.

"Have you not heard, Christine?" she said, with a dramatic shiver. "That opera house is haunted. You could not pay me to work there."

But I do not believe in ghosts, only in music and money. I've never had any money of my own. At the Opera, I will dance, and I will be paid in actual bills and coins that I may spend as I like. I will live and eat in the dormitories at the back of the Opera House, and I will spend my days working and dancing and performing.

I cannot imagine anything more wonderful.

The rotund Monsieur Ricolte is my escort to the city. He is dozing in the carriage, on the bench opposite me. He wakes with a start as the carriage halts before the broad steps of the Opera House. "Ah *merde*. We are here, are we? *Dieu*, but I am stiff after sitting so long. Can you manage your bag, child?"

"Of course. It is only one satchel."

"And you have your papers?"

Despite what he says of his stiffness, I can tell he doesn't want to get out and escort me inside. He wishes to continue on down the street, perhaps to a local inn where he can drink heartily and then sleep before tomorrow's journey back to Marchette.

"I have my papers," I assure him. "Please don't trouble yourself. I'll be fine."

6

"Good, good." He looks briefly uncomfortable, and his jowly face reddens. "Madame Theriault said I should remind you to be wary of men. Especially the kind of men who live and work at an opera house."

Madame Theriault often says such things. Daily she warned us girls of the temptations of men and the wicked allure of our own bodies. She used to walk the school dormitories at night, and if she found any girls with their hands between their legs, she would strike their fingers with a ruler, sometimes hard enough to bruise. I value my fingers for playing piano, so I never risked such naughty explorations.

But I did wonder what physical sensations could be so wonderful that the other girls would risk pain and censure from our headmistress. Perhaps now that I will be living in different quarters, I will have a chance to explore myself.

The thought sends hot blood into my cheeks, which Monsieur Ricolte no doubt interprets as a chaste blush. He nods, relieved. "Good, good. With that warning, I leave you. God watch over you, Mademoiselle."

"And you as well, Monsieur."

With my bag in hand, I hop out of the carriage, waving as it rolls away.

The steps seem to expand, growing wider and wider, stretching farther and farther upward, toward the magnificent peaks and towers and arches, the colonnades and the broad doors of the Opera House.

Gargoyles cluster at the corners of the roof, their mouths open, ready to accept and disgorge rainwater. Tall statues flank the ascending steps—startlingly inappropriate statues of nude men and women, with only bits of flowing stone cloth to hide their privates. A few wear nothing at all. Mentally I compare the lush, weighty breasts of the female statues to my own. Mine are slightly smaller, but of a similar shape.

As I continue mounting the steps, I survey the stone figures with growing interest. One naked statue is holding a lute, and between his legs nestles a diminutive male organ. I have only seen one or two sketches of male parts before. Are they all that small?

"If you're going to ogle him, you should at least buy him a drink first," says a merry voice to my left.

I hastily turn away from the statue, toward the speaker.

It's a young man about my age, with golden waves of hair brushing his shoulders. He's standing on the pedestal of a statue, his lithe body lounging carelessly against the stone arm and breast of a violin-playing Muse.

Despite the gray chill of the afternoon, he's wearing nothing but a pair of blousy, satiny scarlet pants and a metal collar studded with fake gems. Tiny gold caps cover his nipples. His face is strikingly pretty, accented with bronze and crimson paint. A small gold hoop pierces his lower lip.

"Welcome to L'Opera Lajeunesse," he says. "You must be one of our new dancers. I'm Matthieu Giry."

Matthieu carelessly presses a palm over the breast of the stone Muse as he leaps down from the statue's pedestal. "You look lost, *petite chatte*," he says, with a slanted grin.

It's a casual term of endearment, and also a word for some very private feminine parts. My blush returns. "I'm looking for Madame Giry, the woman who manages the dancers?"

"Ah, my illustrious mother. I can take you to her. Though I warn you, if you show up in my company, she might never approve of you. She has never approved of *me*."

"Oh." I am not sure what to say to that. "And you also perform?" I nod to his garb.

"I'm a dancer, yes. A good one, if I say so myself." He rolls his lean body, head to hips, in a way that raises goosebumps over my skin. Thank god I have my cape and long-sleeved gown to conceal the reaction.

I take a moment to steady my expression. "If you would kindly show me where I am supposed to go…"

"Of course, *petite chatte*."

"Please stop calling me that."

He shifts nearer, until I can see every fleck of gold paint on his lashes. He's exactly my height, which puts his mouth precisely on a level with mine. He smells faintly of boyish sweat mingled with traces

9

of vanilla and the familiar powdery scent of ballet chalk.

"Then what shall I call you?" he murmurs. As he waits for a reply, his teeth tug his lower lip, and the late afternoon sun flashes on the gold piercing.

A delicate prickling sensation grazes along the seam between my legs. I have felt such flickers before—the precursor to sinful temptation.

"I'm Christine Daaé," I breathe.

"Christine," he whispers. "You are very new to all this, aren't you, Christine?"

"I've lived at the Marchette School for Girls all my life," I reply. "The city is so big, so overwhelming. And this place—it's enormous."

"It's far larger than anyone knows," he says with a confidential wink. "There are depths, Christine, delightful depths. So much to see, and to learn, and to taste." He flicks his tongue across the lip ring, and when my eyes follow the motion, he chuckles softly. "*Merde*, he is going to love you."

"Who?" I ask, but Matthieu is already bounding up the broad steps, beckoning me to follow him.

Matthieu moves so quickly that I barely have time to take in the enormity, the vast scope of the Opera House. We hurry through huge lobbies with rich red carpets and tall marble pillars, climb staircases with gleaming balustrades, navigate parlors with velvety chairs, and pass by washrooms with shiny sinks. The doors to most of the rooms are open, and the spaces bustle with people polishing the woodwork, brushing the velvet, shifting the chairs, and sweeping the floors.

"Is there a performance tonight?" I ask.

"There is. A small concert. But we are also beginning rehearsals for *La Guerre des Dragons*. You've heard of it? It is about the extermination of the dragons and the expulsion of mages from our country." His upper lip curls a little. "It focuses heavily on the terrifying acts of the dragons, their habit of stealing and sullying maidens—only hinted at, of course, with many a fluttering scarlet cloth to symbolize the act of fornication."

"Mages got their power from the dragons, didn't they?" I've always been curious about the subject, especially since it was one that the Marchette history professor seemed to dislike.

Matthieu lowers his voice. "Mages got their power by forming an intimate connection to the dragons, yes."

"Intimate?"

He smirks and resumes speaking at a normal volume, pushing open a wooden door to reveal a much less luxurious hallway beyond.

"Whatever the historical truth may be, this opera is to be a glorious and garish production, with dozens of dancers, including myself." He bows, indicating his own paint and costume. "I hope you enjoyed your brief passage through the guests' side of the Opera House, Christine, because you'll be spending most of your time back here, in much less glamorous surroundings."

He leads me through a maze of serviceable corridors and plain rooms, occupied by a neverending flurry of laundresses and lamplighters, scene handlers and set painters, ushers and attendants, musicians and dancers. Voices chortle and guffaw, sing and shout, their cacophony blending with the hiss of costumes being steamed, the stamp of dancers practicing in back rooms, the creak of pulleys as set pieces are hauled aside.

"I am sure I will never be able to find my way through all this without a guide," I tell Matthieu.

"It would be my pleasure to offer you guidance anytime you may require it." He casts me a cocky sidelong grin. "Especially if you need a partner for extra practice. I suspect the kind of dancing you've formerly done is a bit different than the kind we do here."

I lift my chin proudly. "The dancing at the Marchette School for Girls focused on elegance, grace, poise, and strength. We performed elaborate routines with complex steps and movements. When the Opera agent came to Marchette to conduct auditions, he was impressed by my skill."

"And your beauty, too, no doubt," says Matthieu. "I don't doubt your skill, but your style may need adjustment. The routine for *La Guerre's* second act requires a certain provocative flair."

I frown, unsure what he means by that. "I assure you I am extremely flexible."

"Are you indeed?" He voices a breathless laugh, tinged with heat. "I look forward to witnessing your flexibility, *ma petite chatte*."

We enter a somewhat quieter space, and he points down a hallway. "Dancers' quarters are that way. Practice rooms and common areas are along here. We just finished a rehearsal, so the dancers will be removing their costumes and returning here to recover from the ordeal, since Maman can be quite exacting and exhausting. She'll be along any moment—ah, there she is now! I shall leave you before she can screech at me for skipping out early from rehearsal. *À bientôt*, Christine. Expect a visitor tonight."

His final words make my belly dip and thrill.

Back at the Marchette School for Girls, boys were a rare sight. They would visit from a nearby gentlemen's academy for spelling competitions and spring promenades, strutting through our school grounds like exotic birds flaunting their plumage. Their only purpose was to help us learn certain aspects of social comportment.

I formed a friendship with only one boy—Raoul, a merry lad with auburn hair and blue eyes. He once plunged into the pond to catch my scarf before the wind carried it away. We saw each other four different times, each one more delightful than the last. I would have liked to see him again, but his parents moved him to a different school.

None of the other boys made me as happy as Raoul did; though after I passed the age of fifteen, I began to find the boys fascinating in a new way. I often felt the soft tickle along my sex when I touched their hands or inhaled their scent—so different from that of girls.

But that attraction was a barely noticeable sensation, a faint warmth, compared to what I feel now, as I watch Matthieu saunter away down the hall.

2

MATTHIEU

I told Christine I was leaving because of my mother's approach, and it was partly true. I don't wish to endure Maman's censorious glare, or tag along while she checks Christine's papers, marches her through the halls, shows her the bunks and showers, and explains the daily schedule. I was raised here. All that is commonplace to me. Boring, even.

But I had another reason for making my escape. I couldn't linger another moment within Christine's space—smelling the delicate honeysuckle fragrance of her hair, watching her luminous golden-brown eyes light up with interest at every new thing I showed her.

I was enchanted by the voluminous curls of her dark brown hair, by the tender notch of her throat, the little dip between her collarbones—I could see that tempting bit of soft skin between the fastening of her cape and the neckline of her dress, and it nearly undid me—*me*, the one in our group who has had the most lovers. I am the youngest, and yet I've slept with more people than Erik or Joseph. Not that I would call myself an expert in matters of fleshly pleasure—

Erik still holds that place in our trio. The very thought of him sends a shudder of dark delight over my body.

But Christine—she is so sweetly innocent, so fresh and pure. She must be a virgin, sequestered as she was at her "school for girls." The thought of seducing her, of luring her to lift those starched skirts and show me her small untouched pussy—I nearly come in my silken pants at the thought.

I force myself to walk around the corner and then I have to pause, brace one hand against the wall, and breathe.

I must think of something unappealing. Ah, of course—the screeching notes and caustic personality of La Carlotta, the opera's prima donna. That should do the trick. Just today, at rehearsal, La Carlotta cuffed a stage handler across the cheek for stepping into her line of sight while she was singing an aria. Rude, arrogant woman. She has mediocre talent and a deplorable personality.

Erik has plans for her downfall, but those plans will only work if he can find an ingenue—someone with natural skill, yet malleable and soft, whom he can bend to his will.

I should have asked Christine if she can sing. All she needs is some raw talent, and Erik can do the rest.

I must tell him about her immediately. If I don't, he will be angry, and an angry Erik is something to be avoided at all costs, unless I'm craving a certain kind of punishment.

There are passages all over the opera house, secret paths linking every part of the building to Erik's haunts down below. I choose one in the back of a storage closet, shifting aside scraps of ancient scenery and popping a wall panel out of place. Stepping through, I snap the panel shut behind me and hurry along the narrow, dusty corridor, cupping one hand over my mouth lest I cough and reveal my presence too soon.

Erik is everywhere and nowhere. He is everyone and no one, a master of disguise and stealth. My heartbeat quickens as I descend a long flight of steps and cut through a tunnel of damp stone.

Ahead I can hear the dim growl of organ music, growing stronger as I approach. I breathe a sigh of relief, because the music means I know exactly where he is, and he won't creep up on me.

I sweep aside a heavy damask curtain and step into Erik's lair—*our* lair, a place of art and music, of candles and books, of magic and sensual pleasure. It is Erik's refuge, but it has become a refuge for Joseph and me as well.

Perhaps one day Christine will join us here. He has been looking for someone like her—a virgin. It is surprisingly difficult to find a virgin of at least eighteen in this dissolute city, and Erik will accept no one younger. He has his own code of honor. A twisted and poisoned code, perhaps, but a code nonetheless.

Lazily I saunter around the organ, trailing my fingertips along the decorative curls of its gleaming gilt edges. The music continues, passionate and intense, dark desire given shape in song.

But when I circle the instrument and glimpse the padded seat, no one is there.

The organ is playing itself.

Before I can react, a noose of silken rope drops over my head and cinches tight, drawing me back against a powerful chest.

I tilt my head back against Erik's cloaked shoulder, fighting every instinct of self-preservation, relaxing into his dominance.

"Matthieu." His voice is deep, rich, and dark.

"Erik. You enchanted the organ."

"You know I am constantly striving to expand my talents."

"I know you're obsessed with being the best at everything. Sculpture, invention, music, magic, architecture, composition—where does it end?"

"It ends when I die," he says. "But next time you catalog my talents, list music first. Music is my ultimate love, Matthieu—you know that."

The noose tightens, restricting my breath slightly. God help me, I'm hard again. Usually I would yield to him and forget all else; but this time, pleasure will have to wait. The news I bear is more important.

"Erik," I wheeze. "I think I've found her. The one we've been looking for."

19

3

CHRISTINE

I cannot sleep. Maybe it is the soft grunting snores from some of the other girls sleeping in the dormitory bunks. Maybe it is the strange smell of this place—hints of paint and chalk, the herbal liniment one dancer applied to her feet, the lingering aroma of the cinnamon cookies another girl passed around secretly before bed—an overindulgence for dancers whose bodies must remain thin and quick.

One of the girls told me I am too full-fleshed, and even Madame Giry advised that I should skip a meal each day. "You have to maintain the same size as the other girls," she said. "You must all be well-matched. You sing? Your headmistress says that you do."

"I do, yes."

"Very good. You will match your voice, tone, and inflection to the other girls in the chorus. Your job is to blend in, to be indistinguishable from the rest, to become one of a seamless whole."

Her words still echo in my head. *Same size, blend in, indistinguishable.*

I thought all I wanted from this role was a place to work, to dance and sing as I love to do, to earn money of my own. But perhaps I want more. To be myself, in the body I choose to have. To stand out from the crowd and be adored above all others. To be truly free, in a way I have never been in my life.

Foolish, prideful dreams.

I should be content here. I am an orphan, with no support and no place in the world. I'm fortunate to have secured this position. I must cling to it with everything I have and give Madame Giry no cause to send me away. It does not matter if the Opera House ends up being yet another cage. Better to live in a comfortable cage than be cast out into the streets.

After turning restlessly in the bed a few more times, I descend from my upper bunk and pad across the wooden floor. The door whines faintly as I slip out into the hallway, but none of the other girls wake or protest.

The long hall is gloomy, lit only by a single lamp near the door to the washroom. I do not need to relieve myself, but I walk there anyway, simply to have something to do.

Matthieu promised me I would have a visitor tonight. I thought that meant he would come to see me, and the hope of it buoyed me through all Madame Giry's recitations of rules and schedules this afternoon. But I have seen or heard nothing of the golden-haired dancer since he left me in his mother's care.

21

As I pause outside the washroom, I hear a faint humming sound, dipping and rising, thin and distant. Someone is singing, and the melody is beautiful.

Charmed, I wander along the darkened hallway, searching for the source of the voice. I peek into empty practice rooms until I reach the corridor's end, where a pair of heavy, paneled doors stand slightly ajar.

Peering inside, I see a small chapel, with a handful of padded pews and an altar at the front. Behind the altar is a stunning statue of a beautiful male angel, naked but for a scrap of artfully placed cloth, with his wings and arms outspread. Flanking the angel are two ornate mirrors, probably to give penitents a chance to look at themselves and reflect on their sins.

Candles burn on a small table before the altar, shedding their glow over the rich wood and crimson carpets. The room smells oddly decadent for a chapel—a heady fragrance of full-blooming roses mixed with the deep musk of cedar, licorice, and pepper. As I creep nearer the altar, I realize that the scent is coming from the candles—tall burgundy tapers with whorls of inky black tracing through the wax.

And the voice which drew me here—it seems to be coming from the statue of the angel. It's a male voice, a perfectly smooth tenor.

My pulse skitters, and my mouth turns dry.

Elise said the Opera House was haunted. If this statue is inhabited by a spirit, it is one I wouldn't mind meeting.

I sink down on the kneeling bench before the altar, bowing my head.

The singing pauses.

"Don't stop," I say quietly. "Your voice is beautiful. Like magic made into melody."

"Flattering child," the voice says softly, and my heart twirls with mingled joy and fear.

"I am no child," I reply. "I am nineteen."

"I thought as much," muses the voice. "Still, it is best to be sure. Do you sing, my dear?"

"I love to sing. Some say I have talent."

"Show me."

I glance backward over my shoulder, at the half-open doors. "What if I wake someone?"

The doors move of their own accord, closing tight.

So I am dealing with a ghost after all. I shiver, and goosebumps travel over my skin. I forgot to pack a nightdress, so I am wearing one borrowed from another girl—a frilly white garment cut low across the chest. Its thin material does nothing to conceal the tightened peaks of my breasts. I cannot see the spirit, but can he see me?

"Sing for me, Christine," says the spirit.

My lungs tighten. "How do you know my name?"

A beat of silence. "I was told your name by someone who cares about your future."

My father must have told this spirit about me. My father is dead, drifting somewhere in the afterlife—hopefully in Heaven—and he has sent this angelic presence to guide me.

"Who are you?" I ask.

"If you sing something for me, I will tell you."

Licking my dry lips, I begin a hymn I was taught by the Marchette chaplain.

With our hearts we worship,
With our souls we trust,
Resting in the hope we
Shall be raised from dust.

When I finish, the male voice laughs lightly, echoing around the chapel until I cannot be certain of its source.

"A pretty tune, and a lovely voice. Tighten your belly as you inhale, to support your lungs. Open your throat for better resonance. And may I suggest a few adjustments to the lyrics?" He begins to sing:

With our mouths we worship
Taking every thrust,
Feeling in our bodies
The sweet glow of lust.

I am not sure what the first two phrases mean, but I know what lust is. It is wrong and wicked. Madame Theriault warned me of it.

"Those words do not seem appropriate," I falter. "Who are you?"

"You may call me 'Angel,'" answers the voice. "An angel of music, who merely wishes to instruct you in the art of song. And the naughty words were a test, sweet one, to discern whether or not your mind has been corrupted. I find it delightfully pure. You are a virgin, yes? No man has touched you in that special place between your legs? Because only a pure-hearted virgin is worthy of my instruction."

He seeks someone pure, untainted by sin; so why do his soft words and rich voice make me feel so wonderfully, wantonly sinful?

"I am untouched," I murmur. "A virgin."

"Ahh," replies the Angel, with an exhale that sounds more hungry than pleased. "Perfect. Let us begin your first singing lesson. Meet me here each night for the next week, and if you do well, I will give you a reward."

For the next seven days, I am caught up in a whirlwind of grueling rehearsals. I barely see the handsome Matthieu Giry, except for brief moments when we are both rehearsing on the main stage. He is in a different group of dancers than I am, so I have little opportunity to speak with him—but we exchange smiles, and he winks at me whenever I pass him backstage.

Every night, I meet with the Angel in the chapel for at least an hour. Sometimes he sings for me, or with me, and I'm astonished at the breadth of his range—from a low rolling bass to a clear, pure soprano. My own range increases as he guides me.

"One day you will sing an E6 for me," the Angel promises. "We will make the sweetest music together, and I will hear you scream in a voice so pure and perfect that the stars themselves shudder in orgasm."

"What is 'orgasm'?" I ask.

Silence hovers in the chapel, and then his voice slithers from the angel statue, curling around me like a living thing. "It is the pinnacle of human pleasure."

I'm standing before the altar, and when he says "pleasure" in that low, warm tone, the crease between my legs tickles again. Perhaps he's speaking of the secret activity Madame Theriault used to punish. "What kind of pleasure?"

"Sexual pleasure. Have you never felt such a thing before?"

"No."

"You have never touched yourself?"

"I was not allowed," I say quietly. "I was hoping to try it when I came here, but I am so tired after rehearsals I can barely stay awake until everyone else is asleep, and then I come here to meet you." My blush grows more intense. "But I am interested in how this pleasure works. You are a spirit, but you seem to know of such things—perhaps you could teach me this as well."

From the vicinity of the angel statue comes a groan so faint I barely hear it.

I tilt my head, listening. "Angel, are you all right?"

"Your purity and innocence is a delight." His voice is slightly hoarser than usual. "I suppose it is best that you learn from a paragon of virtue such as myself, rather than one of these pawing, grunting fools in the theater. Sit on one of the front pews and do as I instruct."

I take a seat on the cushioned pew, knees pressed together, expectant. My skin feels tight and hot.

"Move your legs apart," says the Angel. "Angle yourself to the right—that's it. Now pull up your nightdress, slowly."

I draw the material up my thighs, until my legs and panties are entirely exposed.

The Angel huffs out a sharp breath. "Pull down your panties."

Lifting my hips, I slide the panties along my thighs until they drop to my ankles. The air in the room puffs across my exposed sex. Every tender bit of my flesh feels warm and awake, utterly sensitive.

I should not be doing this. What if someone came into the chapel and found me like this, alone, splayed open? They might think me the worst sort of perverted girl and send me away.

But I do not want to stop.

27

"Spread your legs wider." The Angel's smooth male voice is a little huskier now. "Place the tip of one finger at the top of your sex. There is a small nub there, a very sensitive and delicate place. Touch it, and tell me how you feel."

I reach down between my legs and prod gently at the seam of my folds. He is right; there is a bit of flesh between them, at the top. When I touch it, a sharp zing of pleasure shoots through my lower belly. "Oh," I whisper.

"Tell me how you feel."

"I feel good," I tell him. "As if the inside of my belly is warm and glowing, lit up with a dozen candles. Is that an orgasm?"

He chuckles raggedly. "Not yet. Slide your fingers down, between your inner lips. Do you feel liquid there, Christine?"

As he speaks, I'm obeying him, and suddenly my fingertips are wet. Another ripple of pleasure flows through my flesh, and my head tips back as a sound climbs up my throat—a soft, musical moan.

"I am wet, Angel," I say. "What shall I do now?"

"Draw the wetness upward, over the little bead at the top. Circle it, caress it. Does your body feel tremulous, Christine? Is your pussy so very tender?"

"Yes," I whisper, tracing slick fingers over my sex. "Angel, please—I want something, but I'm not sure what it is. I want more."

"You will have more." His voice is hoarser now, jerking slightly, almost rhythmically, as he speaks.

"You will have all that I can give you, and so much besides. Move your fingers faster, until you feel the pleasure sharpen, and then keep going until it brightens and bursts."

"It is brightening, Angel." I arch my spine, opening my legs wider still. The back of the pew is digging into my shoulder blades, but I don't care. My eyes drift shut, my entire mind centering on the racing motion of my fingers, circling and sliding over my juicy sex. "Oh... oh... I feel as if I want something inside me, Angel."

"You want cock, little one." His voice soothes and seduces me. "You crave a hot, hard cock in that sweet little hole. But not yet. You must give no one your pussy, or I will end our lessons, do you understand?"

"No one will have my pussy," I gasp, my thighs quaking. There's a coiling heat in my body, tightening and surging. "Something is happening, Angel—what is it?"

"You are coming, Christine. Keep tending yourself. Keep—ah—keep going—"

My pulse throbs in my head, in the swollen lips of my sex—my other hand cups my breast instinctively, squeezing. The Angel groans, a rich, rough, beautifully male sound.

The coil in my belly whips outward suddenly, sending lashes of hot pleasure through my body. Every nerve is singing, surging, glowing. Sharp cries break from my mouth, and I convulse on the pew.

Maybe I am dying. If I am, it feels better than I expected.

"*La petite mort*," says the Angel breathlessly, his voice carrying the weight of satisfaction. "'The little death.' It is a sensation worth living for, and to some, worth dying for. Humans have sacrificed kingdoms for that brief moment of ecstasy. That, Christine, was an orgasm."

4

MATTHIEU

When Erik asked me to come to his lesson with Christine, I agreed eagerly. I have not seen her nearly enough since she arrived—I've barely spoken to her, in fact. Erik requested that I keep my distance while he wove himself into her consciousness and earned her trust.

"She needs to feel alone and vulnerable," he said. "Then she will open her heart and mind to me."

"And her legs as well." I winked at him.

He took me by the throat and pressed me to the wall of his lair. My fingers clawed a fistful of tapestry as he ground against my body, his wicked breath hot in my face. "You are not to fuck her," he ordered. "Tell Joseph the same thing. I claim her first. If either of you takes her virginity, I will kill you."

I've seen what he does to those who cross him. So I stayed away from Christine for a full week, and he rewarded me by inviting me to join him for the lesson.

Christine's voice is like starlight, sweet and clear and pure. I listen, entranced, amazed. In the gloom behind the double-sided mirror, Erik grips my knee in a spasm of sheer delight. By the dim glow of the candles filtering through the two-way glass, I can see his expression—utter worship of her beautiful voice. Her talent is beyond what we could have hoped for. It is exactly what we need.

When Erik promises her that she will one day sing an E6, and she asks him what an orgasm is, I reach over and clutch his thigh just as passionately as he gripped my knee, a warning that if he does not take this opportunity, I will die.

Erik is a master of seduction. I remember the first time he persuaded me to pull out my cock for him, the way he teased and tormented me with just two fingers until I came all over his black pants. He manipulates Christine with the same skill; but is it really manipulation if the participant is willing? And clearly she is. The moment she slides off her panties and opens her legs, I can see the glimmer of wetness between the parted lips of her sex.

My body is burning all over and my cock throbs, pushing against my pants with rhythmic twitches. I ease apart the buttons of my trousers and pull my cock out. Erik does the same; he reaches over and strokes my shaft once, affectionately, rubbing his thumb over the head to spread my precum. Then he returns to directing Christine aloud, taking himself in hand as he does it.

He has a massive cock, broad and thick, and I switch between watching him and watching Christine.

Our girl learns quickly, tracing two fingers over her clit, spreading her slit wider and exploring with her fingers.

When she gasps, "I feel as if I want something inside me, Angel," I quiver, my thighs locking and my belly tightening. Erik senses my impending climax and clamps a hand over my mouth.

"You want cock, little one," he says to her, but it feels like he's saying it to me, too. "You crave a hot, hard cock in that sweet little hole."

Heated blood roars to my groin, hardening me even further. My shaft tightens, bobs, and I come hard, splattering the back side of the two-way mirror with my cum, moaning against Erik's warm palm.

Erik holds himself back for another few seconds, but when Christine massages her own breast through her paper-thin nightdress, he comes too, with a harsh groan.

I collapse against Erik's shoulder while he directs Christine to pull up her damp panties again and go to bed. After she leaves, Erik kisses me roughly before saying, "Get some sleep, Matt."

"Why didn't you invite Joseph?" I ask, tucking my cock back into my pants.

"I did," Erik says. "He refused to join us. You should speak to him. I need all of us to be agreed on this. Once I take her the first time, we will be sharing her, if she is agreeable to it. It's the only way to get what we all want—what we need. I do not have time

34

to deal with his moods—I need to prepare for the arrival of the new managers."

"New managers? It is a sure thing, then?"

"Yes. It appears our old friend Mercier is weary of accommodating me and has found a way to escape."

"And you're letting him go?"

Erik touches his mask absently. I am not sure why he wears it every time he comes above ground-level, even when he is well-hidden in secret passageways, even when he's alone with someone like me, who has seen every part of him. But I don't question his choice. Perhaps the mask gives him security.

"Yes, I am letting Mercier go. He has served me well—paid me, accommodated most of my requests, though he still refuses to let me select the productions for the house. Perhaps the new managers will be more amenable. If not, I shall have to persuade them. Now that we have found our ingenue, we can move forward with our plans."

"Why does it always have to be plans?" I moan. "Why can we not simply enjoy her a while?"

Erik takes my face in his hand. "You know why, Matthieu."

"Yes, yes." I sigh. "Very well, I will speak with Joseph. But I make no promises. He barely likes me—tolerates me, like a bothersome little brother."

"But he is not your brother." Erik gives me a rare half-smile.

"No." I lick my lips, remembering certain joint activities between the three of us. "He is not."

5

CHRISTINE

The morning after my first orgasm, I feel strangely hungry. Not for food, but for more of this pleasure. I can think of nothing else. During rehearsal, my costume shifts and ride up between my nether lips a little, and I can barely restrain a gasp. I am newly sensitized, freshly conscious of my body and the wonders of which it might be capable.

During one of our rehearsal breaks, Madame Giry scolds me soundly for my inattention. "You little fool," she hisses. "What has become of your talent? Has it all vanished overnight?"

"No, Madame," I murmur. I notice Matthieu watching me from across the stage, sympathy in his eyes.

"If you cannot keep up with the other girls, you will rehearse until midnight tonight. No dinner. Those clumsy legs of yours could use the practice. Am I understood?"

"Yes, Madame." I bow my head.

She stalks away, and Matthieu approaches me. He is beautiful, with his sleek bare chest gold-dusted and his slim fingers glittering with rings. He looks like a golden-haired dream-prince designed to awaken lust in unsuspecting girls.

"Christine," he murmurs, his lips brushing my curls as he pretends to adjust my headdress. The scent of him is vanilla and amber and heated skin. I lean nearer impulsively, and he draws in a quick breath. "Is my mother being cruel to *ma petite chatte*?"

"A little," I whisper. The titillating friction of my costume is becoming a problem. Dare I adjust it in his presence?

I wriggle a little, trying to rearrange the material in my crotch without actually touching it. My hip bumps lightly against the front of Matthieu's pants.

"*Merde*," he breathes. "Stop that, Christine. You'll make me hard."

"Hard?" I stare at him, not understanding.

"My body will react to yours."

"React?"

"My god, girl, did they teach you nothing about men at that school?"

"Only to stay away from them, and not to let them touch me."

"But you know of sex, yes?"

I look around, desperate. "We cannot speak of this here."

He pulls me aside, into the shadow of a set piece. As I stumble after him, I whimper at the tug of the costume fabric through my folds.

Matthieu stands with his back to the other dancers. They are too busy drinking water and adjusting their footwear to notice us.

"Tell me what you already know," he demands.

I blush fiercely, shaking my head.

"The best way to avoid temptation is to understand it thoroughly," he says, though something in his half-smile warns me he doesn't quite believe what he's saying.

Barely above a whisper, I tell him what I have learned of relations between the sexes. "I know that a man puts his penis into a woman's vagina after they are married, for the purpose of having children."

Matthieu smacks a palm against the set piece, near my head. "There are so many more ways and reasons to have sex. So much pleasure to be had, Christine." His green eyes sparkle with merriment and hunger.

"Pleasure?" My pulse flickers between my legs, and it is all I can do not to touch myself. Sex and orgasms are related then, though it seems one can have an orgasm without sex—without a man at all.

"Pleasure," Matthieu repeats. He gathers a bit of the costume fabric at my waist and tugs. The material pulls tight between my legs, and I inhale sharply.

"Ah," he breathes. "I thought so. Is your costume a little too snug, Christine?"

"It belonged to another girl," I whisper. "Madame Giry said it fits me well enough."

He loosens his hold, then tweaks my costume again. A thrill shoots through my abdomen, and my mouth opens. I'm panting, helpless, trembling in the throes of the same sensations I felt last night.

Matthieu leans in. "What do you want, Christine?"

"More," I whisper. "I want more. I want everything."

But a sharp clapping of hands and a frustrated series of orders makes us both startle. Madame Giry is back, and the break is over.

Hastily I pull the costume material out of the area where it was wedged. I can feel that it's wet now, but I have no time to do anything about it.

I continue to fall short of Madame Giry's standards throughout our dance rehearsal, but when we practice our singing in one of the back rooms, she signals to the other girls to fall quiet while she listens to me.

At first I'm afraid she is going to scold me for not blending well enough with the others in the chorus; but the expression on her face changes as I sing. She almost looks—soft. Kind. Whatever else she may be, it's clear that Madame Giry still holds a deep love for music.

"Very good, Christine," she says. "You have improved in the last week. How did this happen?"

I don't want to answer, but if I refuse I may provoke her anger again. "I've been taking lessons."

"From whom?"

"From—from a private tutor. In my free hours."

She narrows her eyes at me. "A tutor? I was told you were a penniless orphan. How could you afford a tutor?"

"The tutor is a friend of the family. The lessons are free."

"Ah." She looks a bit doubtful, but she nods. "Very well. Continue whatever it is you are doing, and you may soon be Carlotta's equal. Go and wash up for dinner, girls."

I bob a curtsy and hurry off with the others, but secretly my heart is pounding and my very soul is smiling. I always thought my dancing would help me make my way in the world, but what if my voice has power too? What if my song could open even more doors for me?

I must keep taking lessons from the Angel— singing lessons, and perhaps other lessons as well. Matthieu's talk of sex and pleasure has made me very, very curious.

As is our habit, the dancers eat together in the common room. Usually I am closely surrounded by the other girls, but tonight there is more intermingling

42

of the genders. Matthieu takes a seat across the table from me, to the great delight of the girls on either side of him. He chats pleasantly with everyone, but he keeps catching my eye.

A young man with brown skin and a burly, muscled frame enters with a message for one of the dance managers. When the instructor leaves, the girls around me call out to the messenger, "Stay, Joseph, stay! Tell us a story—a frightening one!"

The young man's broad lips stretch in a gentle smile, and his brown eyes sparkle with mischief. He tosses aside the locs of black hair that have tumbled over his forehead. "You lot have already heard all my stories."

"Tell us one we've heard then," calls a boy. "The one about the Phantom of the Opera!"

"Oh yes! The Opera ghost!" cries another. "Tell us that one, Joseph!"

"You want that one?" Joseph looks around at the eager faces. "Right." He turns a chair backward and sits astride it, his arms lying across the back.

I find myself fascinated by those sinewy brown forearms and his thick, strong fingers. His face is a delight, too—wide, handsome features softened by the glow of the firelight.

"No one knows where the Opera ghost came from," he says. "Some say he was a builder who seduced some rich lord's wife, that he was killed and buried in the foundation. Some say he was cursed for some foul sin and wandered into the Opera while it was being constructed—and he never left. Others say he was a guest who went mad. But they all agree on one thing."

Joseph pauses, and silence shivers in the room, thin and brittle.

"His face," says Joseph, in his deepest tones. "Skin like crinkly parchment spotted with mold. A gaping hole where his nose should be. Eyes sunken deep, so deep they are merely specks of hellish light in two hollow caves. Teeth crooked and rotted, and a tongue forked down the center."

The girls around me squeal and clutch each other. I stare at Joseph, enraptured and horrified. The spirit in the chapel—is it the Opera ghost? Or are my Angel and the ghost distinct from each other? Is the ghost truly as hideous as they say?

Joseph spins a lurid tale of the Opera ghost haunting the dreams of a stagehand. The dance instructor returns in the middle of the story, right when the ghost is pulling down the stagehand's trousers while he sleeps.

"Joseph, hold your tongue," barks the instructor. "Boys, enough of this. Back to your dormitory. If Madame Giry heard you corrupting her girls, she would have me tan your bare asses with a stick."

"Promises, promises," mutters Matthieu. Joseph half-chokes on a laugh as he leaves the common room.

"Corrupting us," titters one of the girls as we rise from the table. "What does he know? All of us are thoroughly corrupted by now, isn't that right, Matthieu?" She pokes out her pink tongue at him, and he laughs.

Unhappiness twinges inside me when I think of him leaning close to her instead of me, touching her waist instead of mine.

But it is a foolish feeling. Matthieu is a friend. As the newest dancer and chorus girl, I cannot risk any romantic attachments or other entanglements.

Though perhaps I am already entangled, in ways I did not suspect until it was too late to stop it. Not that I want to stop the strange, sensual journey I seem to be undertaking.

In the bustle that follows, while everyone else is carrying their dinner dishes to the kitchen cart and bidding each other good night, I slip out of the common room and run after Joseph Bouquet. My curiosity about the Opera ghost is too powerful. I must find out if Joseph is making everything up, or if he knows something real.

"Monsieur Bouquet," I call.

He is nearly to the end of the hall, but he turns immediately, a quizzical look on his face. "No one calls me 'Monsieur Bouquet.' I am only twenty-two. How old are you, girl?"

"Nineteen."

"And what do you want?"

"I was wondering—that is, I was curious—have you heard the voice of the Phantom, the Opera ghost? Do you know what he sounds like? Is his voice more creaky and ancient, like an old man, or whispery and wild, or do you think it could possibly be a beautiful voice…" My words trail off as he stares at me.

All traces of humor and mischief are gone from his face now. "What is your name?"

"Christine Daaé."

"Fuck," he says, and my heart jumps into my throat at the foul word. I know it is foul, because once a servant said it near a group of us young ladies at Marchette, and Madame Theriault overheard him. The servant was fired that very day. The headmistress and Madame Giry are similar in many ways.

Joseph must notice the widening of my eyes, because he winces and shakes his head. Somewhere behind me, a clatter of feet and a stir of merry voices announces the exit of everyone else from the common room. Joseph catches my elbow and pulls me around the corner, down a few steps to a short hallway swathed in darkness. He pushes me against the wall.

"You stay away from the ghost, you hear me? Have nothing to do with ghosts, spirits, angels—"

"What do you know of angels?"

"I know enough." He's so much taller than me. I can sense the power of his body even though I can barely see the outline of him in the gloom. He smells of baked bread, of sage and parsley, savory and fresh at once.

"You smell delicious," I murmur. "Do you work in the dormitory kitchens?"

"Sometimes. I enjoy cooking." Then he makes a frustrated sound and grips my chin. "Don't try to befriend me, Daaé. Avoid Matthieu as well, if you know what's good for you, and speak to no spirits."

"But the spirit knows things that I want to know," I counter. "So does Matthieu. Why would you warn me against both of them? Unless they are connected somehow—are they?"

"Fuck," he says again, fervently.

"Tell me what that word means," I whisper.

"No. You should go to your dormitory." But he steps closer, his burly frame caging mine. There's a sucking, thrumming tension all along the lines of my body, pulling my limbs to his. I have the strangest sense that this handsome cook, this muscled teller of stories, is connected to the Angel and to Matthieu somehow—connected to everything.

I tilt my face up to Joseph's. "Tell me what the word means, and I'll go to bed."

My eyes are adjusting to the dark, and I can make out an aggrieved expression across his features. But there's something else, too, the same hunger I recognized in Matthieu's eyes—a longing that is echoed deep in my core. Here in the shadows, the desire inside me unfurls, ravenous now that it has been released.

Joseph sweeps his thumb across his lower lip.

"What does 'fuck' mean?" I murmur.

47

"You're not innocent at all, are you?" he growls. "You're a pretender, faking virginity when you're really a damn succubus. There is no way a naïve girl plays with a man like you're playing with me. Admit it—you've been fucked before."

I draw back a little. "What?"

"Fucked. Rutted. Had sex. Taken a cock between your legs."

"No," I say faintly. "None of those things."

He vents a groan of frustration and plants both hands on either side of my head. "Liar. Have you been kissed by a man before?"

"No…"

"There's only one way to know if you're telling the truth," he mutters, and then he's kissing me.

6

JOSEPH

It's immediately clear that Christine Daaé has never been kissed.

Her mouth stays soft, pliant, and motionless under mine. Her lips tremble a little, but she doesn't seem to know what to do with them. The tentative sweetness of her makes my cock stiffen and twitch.

I see now why Erik and Matthieu are so enamored with her. When Matthieu came to speak to me about it, I tried to dissuade him from this. Luring an innocent girl into the web of darkness we've woven feels wrong to me. I told him and Erik I wouldn't be a part of it.

That's why I'm warning her to stay away. Warning her—by kissing her?

God. What is wrong with me? I pull back at once.

Christine looks dazed and delighted.

"So you weren't lying," I say gruffly. "You haven't had a man before. Not even a kiss."

"Am I that terrible at it?" She winces.

"You'll get better with practice."

"So you'll teach me?"

"No! No, I didn't say that. I'm warning you, remember? Stay away from them—from us. No good can come from associating with lecherous men or deceptive spirits."

I force myself to move away from her, but she catches my sleeve. "Wait! I feel as if there's so much I need to know—so much I haven't been told. Like I've stepped into a world that I don't understand. Please, answer my question. The Opera ghost in your stories—is he as horrific as you said?"

My hands roll into fists. "In his own way, yes."

It feels like I'm betraying Erik. If my words cause her to pull away from him, there will be consequences. He will mete out heavy punishment on my head, or perhaps other parts of my body. But Christine seems like a good girl—perhaps a little too hungry for forbidden knowledge, but *good*. Too good for us. Too sweet and sensitive to endure what Erik has planned for her.

I jerk my sleeve out of her grasp and leave the shadowy recess, striding down the hall, trying to forget how her lips felt like rose petals under mine, how a sliver of her breath ghosted over my mouth as I pulled away. In that moment I could feel her body pulling me toward her, a compelling force exerted over my skin, my flesh, my very bones. I craved the crush of our bodies, wanted to claw her against me and devour all of her.

After my last dalliance with a chorus girl ended badly, I determined not to bed anyone for a while. I haven't been with Erik and Matthieu in weeks, and I've hardly found time to take myself in hand. The pent-up lust is roaring through me now, burning in my belly.

I walk faster, desperate to get to my tiny closet of a room near the back kitchens. It's a spidery, drafty space no one else wanted, but I don't care about the cold or the creatures—I like having a place that is all mine, rather than being shoved into a bunkhouse with the other stagehands or having shared rooms somewhere in the city and trekking to work every day.

A lithe shape whisks in front of me—golden hair and the scent of vanilla. Matthieu presses a hand to my chest, stopping me in my tracks.

It is late, and we are alone in this corridor.

"Well?" His eyebrows lift. "Did you speak with her?"

I growl and try to push past him, but he shifts his body, his chest brushing mine, blocking my way.

"You *did* speak with her. What did you think? Is she not everything we could have dreamed? Beautiful, innocent, nubile, eager, and her voice—exquisite. She can be our anchor, Joseph. Just think of it."

"She's too young, too naïve," I protest. "She cannot handle what we we'll ask of her."

"She is already full of questions," Matthieu retorts. "She is ravenously curious about sex, hungry for the sins of the flesh. Of course Erik will take her first—but think of the power he'll have afterward—power he can share with us."

"And that is all you care about. Power."

"*Mai oui*, Joseph!" he exclaims, frustrated. "I've lived my entire life in this Opera House, without a shred of power to call my own. My mother's heavy hand has always been on my shoulder, shoving me into the art of dance, pushing me to train until my feet bled. This is my life, and I cannot see it ever being any different. When I am too old to be a dancer, I'll be a stagehand like you, until I die."

"And that would be such a terrible fate, being like me."

Matthieu fists a handful of my shirt. "Don't you want more than this? More than cooking meals and shifting props and pulling on ropes? More than scaring silly girls with ghost stories?"

"I am content," I say.

"Well, I am not. I want more."

"What you want is dangerous. But you and Erik never seem to stop and think about the peril."

"I do," Matthieu replies. "I even asked Erik if we could just enjoy the girl for a while, before we move ahead with his *plans*. But no. He does not listen to me. Maybe he would listen to you."

"He will get us all killed if he is not careful," I mutter. "*La Guerre des Dragons*, Matt. What happened to them—it could happen to us."

"You think I don't know that? You think *he* doesn't know?" Matthieu vents a frustrated sound.

"But it's better than this sameness, Joseph, this nothing. I would rather live and *choose* than continue to be controlled by everyone else. I've never chosen anything in my life, except this—" he points to his lip ring— "and Erik, and—and you."

His hand still grips my shirt. I tense, every nerve in my body ringing with suppressed need.

"I know you don't like me," he whispers. "You find me annoying, even when you're fucking me."

"That's not true."

"It is. But I don't care. I can bear your dislike as long as I know we're still connected. Not just to Erik, but to each other."

His words touch something deep inside me. As much as he hates his mother's control, I would give anything to have one family member, one relative. Matthieu and Erik are all I have, my only real friends, my partners. Maybe I haven't been clear about what they mean to me.

Taking a cue from him, I snag a handful of his loose shirt and pull him up on his toes, nudging my profile against his. "You want to be connected to me, Matthieu?"

"Yes," he breathes, and I swallow the word with a kiss. I consume him, inhaling his breath, drinking the tiny moan he releases. When he slips his tongue into my mouth, I suck on it gently, until he bucks his body against mine. Our cocks grind together beneath our pants, roll on roll of hard flesh.

He and I have only been together with Erik involved, or at least with him watching. Erik is always watching. But tonight, part of me wants it to be just me and Matthieu, linked by some deep-seated pain that we're both trying to speak through our bodies, by a need that jolts through our blood and gives itself voice in our passionate groans.

Somehow we manage to break apart and walk side by side to my closet of a room. Matthieu doesn't turn up his nose at the surroundings. He pushes down my pants with desperate force and runs my length into his mouth. I nearly roar as the smooth metal nub of his lip ring skims the sensitive underside of my cock. Just a few pumps of his mouth, a gentle squeeze to my balls, and I'm shaking, surging into his throat, my cum flowing into him.

He swallows and looks up at me with a beautiful smile on his face, his lips and cheeks wet. And then I lay him on my bed, and I give him head in return, using every technique Erik has taught me.

When it's over, I kiss him with lips salty from his own skin. "If this is really what you need, I will help you and Erik. I will do whatever it takes to bring this girl into our group. I want her too. But more than that, I want you to be happy. Even if you do annoy me."

Matthieu laughs. "How kind of you. The new managers of the theater arrive soon, and I think Erik will make a move then. He hasn't told me what, of course—you know how he is—but we should both be ready for anything."

7

MATTHIEU

I'm dancing better than ever today. The moments Joseph and I shared loosened something inside me—or maybe secured it. I feel free to move in a way that I haven't for weeks. Perhaps it's the knowledge that both Christine and Joseph are stealing glances at me despite being occupied with their own work—she with her dancing and he with the set pieces.

We're doing another full dress rehearsal today, since our first performance of *La Guerre des Dragons* is in just three nights. Our conductor, Maestro Trovato, seems more frustrated than usual, perhaps because our diva Carlotta keeps missing her marks onstage and then screaming at the dancers as if it is their fault.

Our tenor, Piangi, is usually oblivious to Carlotta's moods despite the fact that they share a bed. In his eyes, she can do no wrong. However, even he has noticed her heightened irascibility today. He keeps trying to soothe her by cooing little pet names in between his lines—another factor in the Maestro's frustration.

I find it all very amusing, especially given the fact that, if Erik's information is correct, the new managers will be arriving within the hour. There could not be a better stage set for what the Opera Ghost has planned. I know my role, and Joseph knows his. Now we simply need Carlotta to be her vain, obnoxious self, and we need our little ingenue to follow the cues as they're given to her.

Christine is dancing and singing beautifully, every step perfectly synchronized with the others. After so many years of learning an elegant, restrained style of dance, I wondered how she would adapt to the more seductive style required for this performance, but she has laid all my doubts to rest. Her body has an inborn sensuality to its lines. She is pliant, graceful, and unconsciously erotic in her movements.

Her singing is excellent, too; not a single phrase falters on her lips. I even notice her mouthing along to some of Carlotta's lines. She was born for the stage, though she may not yet know it. An agile mind and body, a retentive memory, a thirst for knowledge, both artistic and sensual—she is a dream. She is *my* dream. Our dream.

My heart throbs, warm and soft, in my chest, and I have to look away from her or I might explode with joy. I let my emotions flow through the dance, energizing my limbs.

Despite my mother forcing me into dancing as a career, I truly do love it. Perhaps not the hours of practice, but I appreciate the result—the keen reflexes, the power of my body, its grace, partly natural and partly earned. I leap, sway, bow, and bend along with the others, until suddenly our manager Mercier walks onto the stage and waves his arms, calling for a halt to the dress rehearsal.

"Monsieur Mercier, pardon," objects Maestro Travato. "We are rehearsing. We must not be stopped, for there is much to do. Too much to do." He wipes his sweating forehead, looking thoroughly peeved and panicked.

"You must excuse the interruption, Maestro, it could not be helped," says Mercier. "I am here to announce that I am retiring. These gentlemen are the new managers of L'Opera Lajeunesse. Monsieur Firmin Richard and Monsieur Armand Moncharmin. Please make them welcome."

"New managers?" says the conductor feebly, and Carlotta begins to swear profusely, words I'm sure our little Christine has never heard in all her sheltered life. When I glance at Christine, she looks positively intrigued. I look back over my shoulder, into the shadows offstage where Joseph watches. I grin at him, thinking about what he told me of their conversation—how she asked him to explain the word "fuck." She'll have a number of new words to ask him about after this.

Joseph also told me that he kissed her, and honestly I'm a little jealous he tasted her mouth first. I'm not sure how Erik will react once he finds out.

Our former manager is hastening everyone into their places again, requesting that we continue rehearsal so the new managers can see what they've purchased. My mother pulls the managers aside, pointing out various members of the cast while Monsieur Mercier recedes into the background, clearly hoping to make his final exit sooner rather than later.

I suppose he is glad to be rid of the theater and of Erik. The Opera Ghost has been more mischievous than usual over the past few months, particularly where Carlotta is concerned. Erik enjoys slinking along the beams above the stage and sending various items crashing onto the boards—near misses that startle the diva into some very ungainly notes. He also likes to misplace her props, unravel the hems of her costumes, and draw male genitalia on her dressing room mirror. All of which has enraged her mightily, more so because Mercier is too frightened of Erik to take any action against him. The theater manager and the Phantom of the Opera House have had an arrangement between them for a long time. No doubt Erik terrorized him into agreeing to the salary and certain other accommodations.

I'm not sure the new managers will be so easily manipulated.

The rehearsal is about to resume, but I take a moment to join my mother, on pretense of greeting the new managers.

"Ah, Matthieu." My mother's stiff smile communicates a clear rebuke. *Why are you out of place? Back to your mark!* But she manages to say politely, "Messieurs, this is my son Matthieu, one of our male dancers."

"A pleasure." I grin at them, letting the tip of my tongue trace my lip ring—an adornment my mother detests and barely tolerates. Neither of the men react except with mild interest and acknowledgement. They both enjoy women, then. Which gives me all the information I need to perform the part Erik set for me.

"We need fresh chalk for the shoes, and no one has refilled the tray," I tell my mother. "And one of the soldiers' costumes is unraveling."

"*Merde.* Excuse me, gentlemen." She hurries away.

"We have some of the best ballet and chorus girls in the country here at L'Opera Lajeunesse," I tell the two men. And then, more confidentially, I murmur, "With the loosest morals, as well. You see that one? And the blonde? And the girl with the brown curls? Always ready to play, they are. Watch the girls closely, and if they wink at you, they're asking for a good time."

With another grin I hurry back to my mark, before my mother can return and scold me for the false alarm about the chalk and the costume.

Rehearsal begins, and I'm pleased to witness the results of my sly words. Our two new managers are ogling the dancing girls and ignoring Carlotta entirely. Monsieur Mercier knew when to give his leading lady his full attention, and thanks to me, these men haven't so much as glanced her way during the entire aria.

Carlotta sways more vigorously and raises her voice, her full-throated vibrato nearly shaking the stage. Still Messieurs Richard and Moncharmin pay her no mind, only lick their lips and smirk at the half-naked girls prancing and slithering within arm's reach.

As the aria ends, Carlotta voices a final desperate screech. Monsieur Mercier startles and dashes away to a side exit, while Richard and Moncharmin finally take notice of the diva, giving her half-hearted smiles.

"Magnificent," says Moncharmin vaguely.

Carlotta is about to respond when the lamps above the stage all go out at once, plunging the theater into blackness.

My gasp isn't feigned—I am astonished every time I witness Erik's abilities. The power he has now is only a fraction of what he could possess.

Screams erupt from the dancers, and objects crash onto the planks of the stage. My mother's voice rises, begging everyone to be calm.

A whisper of wind races through the theater, as if something has passed—or flown—over our heads.

And then the lights wink on once more, illuminated as if by magic.

By magic, indeed.

Cries of "The Opera Ghost! The Phantom!" ripple through the cast, reaching the managers' ears.

63

They look incredulous—and then shocked as they take in the sight of Carlotta.

She's patting her forehead. "I thought I felt something crawling on my face in the dark!" she cries, shuddering.

When she moves her hand, everyone can see that a large dick and testicles have been scrawled above her brows in charcoal. All around her lie chunks of debris, including a lamp bracket.

"My—my dear, your face," the tenor Piangi murmurs nervously. "Allow me to wipe it."

"No!" screams Carlotta. "No! This theater has no respect for talent. This Opera Ghost—he is just an excuse for vile stage workers like that one—" she points to Joseph— "to play terrible jokes with the lights, dangerous jokes with the scenery."

"I did nothing, Messieurs, I swear," says Joseph. "I was standing right here the whole time. My crew and I were as much in the dark as you—we did nothing."

Nothing that anyone could prove, of course. But thanks to Erik, Joseph and I both have access to very small amounts of magic, and Joseph used his to see in the dark and draw on La Carlotta's face.

"You did nothing, eh?" squawks Carlotta. "While we are speaking of doing nothing—that little shit Mercier *did nothing* to stop these pranks, these 'accidents'—and you two seem just as useless—leering at the dancers like puerile boys."

The two managers try to keep their composure, but the charcoal penis on the diva's face proves too much for them both, and they have to smother a chuckle. Which is, of course, disastrous, exactly as we planned.

The soprano practically shrieks with fury. "I am La Carlotta, light of the fucking stage, and I will not be mocked. Nor will I sing under these conditions!"

She gathers her voluminous skirts and marches away, probably thinking she cuts a grand figure making her exit. But the dick on her forehead rather mars the effect.

And now the harsh reality sets in. I can see it registering on the faces of the managers.

"What will we do?" they say, glancing around for Mercier. But he is gone for good. Maestro Travato only shrugs despairingly, and even my mother is speechless.

"Is there an understudy?" asks Moncharmin.

The maestro shakes his head. "Carlotta would not allow it."

"We have no star," says Richard, with the dull horror of a man who is just realizing what he has done. "And opening night is in three days."

The new managers will lose a vast amount of money if they have to cancel the first performance and refund the price of every ticket. They will be ruined before they begin.

It is time for me to step forward again, because with all the dramatics, no one has noticed the large envelope lying on the floor near the managers' feet.

"What is that?" I say loudly. "That red wax seal—it looks like a skull!"

Two of the girl dancers clutch my arms and quiver against me. "Opera Ghost," they whimper, delighted and terrified.

Moncharmin picks up the letter. "It is addressed to us," he says, with an apprehensive look at Richard. Breaking the seal, he reads Erik's message.

Delighted to make your acquaintance, Messieurs. I hope you will be pleased with the Opera Lajeunesse, though I am sure you will agree with me that certain changes need to be made. Our partnership may begin immediately, starting with the delivery of my salary (in the amount inscribed below), which may be left on the center seat in Box 5 on the night of the first performance of "La Guerre des Dragons." As Monsieur Mercier should have told you, Box 5 is to be left always open for me, that I might enjoy the performances at my leisure. I will have further requests to make of you, but we shall begin with these two small things, which, if you accomplish them aptly, shall be a promising presage of our future cooperation. I remain yours respectfully, The Phantom of the Opera.

"What is this?" squawks Moncharmin, lifting the letter. "What the hell is this? Which of you wrote this?"

"It is clear," says Richard in a quavering tone, "that this theater is infested with the most unprofessional pranksters. Rest assured that we will not stand for it. We will rout them out with all possible speed so that our performances may continue unhindered."

"Performances?" the maestro interrupts, nearly in tears. "What performances, messieurs? We have no one to sing the lead roles."

"We still have Piangi." Richard points to the tenor, who has been pacing agitatedly, clearly unsure whether he should remain or follow Carlotta.

"I will sing if she allows me," Piangi says, with a desperate shrug.

"But he is no leading lady," says Moncharmin. "And there is no understudy for Carlotta!"

Again I step forward. "There is one other option, Messieurs. On this very stage is a young woman who knows both the libretto and the melody. Someone with a lovely voice—Christine Daaé."

My mother shoots daggers at me with her eyes, but I fix her with the most intense look I can manage, the one I use when I'm deadly serious. "You know she can sing it," I say. "Tell them."

"Can she, Madame Giry?" asks Moncharmin.

My mother pinches her lips together, then nods. "She is a great talent, and she has been taking lessons. I believe she could manage it."

"At least let her audition for the role," I continue. "Right here, right now."

Christine is staring at me, her brown eyes wide with shock, excitement, and fear.

I give her an encouraging nod.

"This is a very bad idea," groans Richard, but Moncharmin sighs and says, "What choice do we have? Sing for us, child."

 CHRISTINE

At the Marchette School for girls, music was a balm, a refuge, and a delight for me. I could retreat into it when I needed comfort, relish it when I required an outlet for all the passion surging inside me. I loved practicing alone, worshiping music with my body or my voice, almost as much as I adored performing for the other students or for the occasional group of distinguished guests who visited the school.

Performance is frightening, but invigorating, too—like my interactions with the young men I have met, Joseph and Matthieu. Like my meetings with the Angel.

But when the theater managers ask me to sing an aria I have never practiced, in front of the entire cast, the stagehands, and everyone else involved in the rehearsal, I do not feel invigorated. I feel absolutely terrified.

The maestro gives a helpless shrug and leads the orchestra in the introductory notes of the song.

Matthieu Giry is watching me, his green eyes sparkling with a challenge, his smile warm with encouragement.

His mother, Madame Giry, gives me a little shove forward. Like my headmistress at Marchette pushing me out of the nest. This is simply one more drop into the unknown, one more fall to see if I might fly.

My voice wavers a little as I begin to sing, and the managers mutter unhappily to each other. But then I think of something my Angel of Music told me one night, during a lesson.

"The song is already inside you, Christine," he said. "You simply need to let it out, and to follow it. Your beautiful voice yearns to be free, and you have only to release it. If the size of your audience overwhelms you, know that there is someone waiting to hear that song, the way you alone can sing it. If you are still frightened or uncertain, pretend that I am listening, and sing just for me. Because I will always hear you."

The Angel, the spirit, the Phantom of the Opera—perhaps he can hear me now.

I let my voice flood from my very soul—I release it, and I follow it as it soars. I use my breath to support every note, smooth and steady as the Angel taught me. I keep my throat open, shape my mouth, my tongue, my palate and my lips for precise diction and for the unfettered passage of my voice, my glorious voice.

It doesn't feel vain to admit the glory of my performance. My voice was always good, yes, but it has become truly exceptional since I came here, since the Angel of Music began to teach me. He unlocked something in my mind and my body—a passion that fuels my song.

When the aria ends, and I let the final note trail into silence, quiet envelops the theater.

And then Joseph Bouquet, standing just offstage, smacks his broad palms together and begins to clap, his face tight with some fierce emotion. The other stagehands, the dancers, the extras, the footmen, the women dusting the seats—even Piangi, Madame Giry, and the managers—they all start clapping too.

"It is settled!" cries Monsieur Moncharmin. "Christine Daaé shall take the lead in Carlotta's place! Get her fitted for a costume and start the rehearsal again, from the beginning!"

The next several hours are packed with work, with lines I must learn and notes I must achieve, with choreography to master and new marks to find when I'm onstage. I've been watching Carlotta closely, and we've practiced so many times I already know most of her lines. Still, by the end of the day I am exhausted.

My things have been moved to a different room—not Carlotta's room, but a chamber with its own privy. The managers insisted that their new star needed privacy and rest. I think they are terrified of losing another soprano. They do not know that I would be content to stay in the dormitories.

For an orphan like me, someone who has always shared space with other girls, a private bedroom is an astounding luxury. After closing the door, I poke my head into the wardrobe and check all the drawers, wishing I had more than a few possessions to put in them.

My bed is against the far wall, with its foot near a large gilt-framed mirror that reminds me of the ones in the chapel. In fact, this room is not far from the chapel, tucked away at the end of a long, dimly-lit corridor. I can rehearse privately if I like, and I doubt anyone in the dormitory rooms could hear me.

I remove my outer clothing and lie on the bed, dressed in my corset, my panties, and the garters and stockings I wore under my costume today.

The corset and panties are new, not my regular ones—these are pure white, beautifully designed from soft fabrics and edged with lace. Shortly after I was named the new leading lady, Joseph Bouquet delivered the underclothes to the dressing room in a box tied with black ribbon, with a red rose tucked against the lid.

"From the managers, for their new star," he said. When he looked at me, I felt the heat of his gaze all along my body. "They request that Miss Daaé wear these for rehearsal, and keep them afterward."

The woman in charge of costumes seemed surprised. "How very scandalous," she said. But she touched the pieces admiringly and helped me into them after Joseph left.

I like the underthings so much I do not want to take them off. The corset supports my breasts, pushing them up without being uncomfortable, and the panties are so silky—I can't resist touching them.

I half-sit, propped against the pillows so I can see myself in the mirror at the foot of the bed. I watch my fingers trail across the silken material between my legs.

My whole body is murmuring with warm, languid desire. I wish the Angel of Music were here to show me how I should touch myself again. Perhaps I can remember enough to do it alone.

Before I can try it, a faint voice begins to sing, its gentle melody circling me, suffusing the air of my room. I know that heavenly male voice.

My Angel has found me.

"Well done, little one," he says. "Your talent and my teaching have been honored today."

"You know about my new role?" I scan the room for any sign of him—a glow, a wisp of mist, anything. But all I can hear is his beautiful voice.

"I know everything, dear one," he says. "I heard you singing for me today, and it gave me such pleasure."

"Did it give you an orgasm?" I whisper.

"An orgasm for the ears, yes." He chuckles. "Are you ready for your lesson?"

"I have sung so much today," I tell him. "My voice is tired. Could we have a different kind of lesson instead?"

"What did you have in mind?"

"I thought perhaps you could teach me again about the little bead of pleasure, and how to make it sing."

"It is called your clitoris," he says. "And yes, I would be happy to teach you more of self-pleasure, as long as you swear to me that you will keep yourself pure. Do not let any man touch you."

I hesitate, remembering how Joseph kissed me in the shadows, how he warned me to stay away from him, from Matthieu, and from the spirit.

"Has someone touched you?" says the Angel sharply.

"Only a kiss." I touch my lips. "A handsome stagehand named Joseph kissed me. And he warned me to stay away from spirits like you."

"Did he now?" The Angel's voice is harder, almost stern.

"Forgive me, sweet Angel," I plead. "When I was on that stage today, I thought of you, and it strengthened me. I know you have my best interests at heart. You are my guardian, my guide. My protector and my teacher. I am so grateful to you. From now on I will reserve my lips, my voice, all of me, for you alone."

His tone softens. "That pleases me so much, Christine. And now, my lamb, to your lesson. Remove your panties."

I slip them off and drop them over the edge of the bed.

"Arch your knees and spread your thighs," he directs.

I obey, fully opened, seeing my entire pussy in the mirror. My inner folds gleam with moisture.

"There is preparation we must do, widening your vagina in the same way that you widen your throat so the notes may pass through easily."

"What will be passing through my vagina?" I ask, though I know the answer. I want him to say it.

"Eventually, when you are ready and when I allow it, you will have a man's cock in that sweet small hole," he says.

Something about his words makes me shiver with slight apprehension and close my thighs. "Can you see me right now, Angel?"

A pause. Then, "Do you want me to see you, lamb? Do you want to know that I'm watching you pet your pretty little pussy?"

My stomach thrills. My entire lower belly is awash with tingling warmth, pulsing stronger at the tiny peak that he called my clitoris.

"Yes," I whisper, opening my legs again. "I want you to watch me, Angel."

He is a spirit, so he cannot react to me the way that Matthieu mentioned—a hardening of his body. But perhaps the Angel finds some pleasure in watching me. And I want to bring him pleasure.

I relax against the soft pillows, inhaling the faint scent of roses from the vase on the dresser. Even without a fireplace, this room is warm, and the blanket I'm lying on is the softest I've ever felt. My skin feels perfectly, wonderfully alive.

"I want to please you, Angel," I murmur. "Tell me how."

"Trace the outer lips of your sex," he says. "Push them slightly apart. Like that, yes. Now slide two fingertips through your inner folds. Good girl. Ah, you are soaked, Christine. Lift those wet fingers to your nose and inhale for me. That is your scent. Your scent belongs to me."

I smell faintly sweet. Experimentally I put my two fingers into my mouth and suck on them.

A sharp inhale from the Angel. "What are you doing?"

"Tasting."

"God," he says fervently. "Touch your pussy again, Christine. This time, press one finger into your slit. Do not go too far inside. Now a second finger."

I nudge both fingers a little way into my hole. There's a tugging tightness, but it doesn't hurt. I fight the urge to push farther inside. I am so wet that, at the Angel's direction, I am able to insert a third finger a few moments later. He makes me hold them there awhile, while he tells me how some men like to lick and suck a woman's parts.

"That must feel wonderful." I'm trembling, my body leaking copious amounts of slippery fluid around my fingers. "Angel, may I touch my clitoris now?"

"Yes, you may touch your clit, Christine. Wiggle it for me, my sweet lamb, my good girl. Tell me how it feels."

Before he finishes speaking, I'm rubbing my clit wildly, gasping at the spikes of pleasure that race through my belly. My skin is on fire, flames licking the length of my spine, my mind a searing blur of lust. "Oh Angel, the orgasm is coming!"

"Spread your legs wider," he pants. "I want to see you come. You must move your hand away exactly when I tell you."

"Yes," I sob, jiggling my clit faster. "Yes. Oh yes, Angel!" A bolt of exquisite pleasure shears through me and I squeal, bucking against the bed.

"Move your fingers," barks the Angel, and I whip my hand away from my sex, gripping my thighs, holding them apart. I desperately want to keep touching my pussy while it spasms, but I must obey the Angel.

He's moaning softly. "Just like that. You are so wet, so perfect, so beautiful. You are *mine*."

"Yours," I echo. "I belong to you."

The Angel cries out so sharply that at first I think he must be in pain. But then I realize that his cry isn't pain at all; it sounds rather like mine when I came. A cry of pleasure.

What if the Angel is not a spirit at all, but a man hiding somewhere in this room? Behind the walls maybe? His voice is always a little distant, a little muffled.

The idea scares me briefly, but spirit or man, he is still my tutor, my guardian, my instructor in music and pleasure. And if he is a real man, then he must have real hands and a real cock. He could touch me with those hands. He could put that cock inside me.

I think I would like that.

"I must go," he says, and though his voice is calm, there is a tremor in it, the way the earth might shudder in the aftershocks of a great quake. "There is someone else I must visit tonight."

"Are you going to see Joseph?"

Silence.

"I'm not a fool," I tell him. "I know you are angry with him for kissing me, and for warning me about you. Do not hurt him, please."

"What makes you think I would hurt anyone?"

"I've heard the stories everyone tells. You've hurt people before, haven't you, with your ghostly tricks? Bumps and bruises, mostly, but they say if there's a dancer who doesn't perform to a certain standard, they mysteriously end up with sprained ankles or other injuries that force them to quit the Opera."

"I never harm anyone without a reason," he replies, and as I begin to speak again he cuts me off. "You are new to this place, Christine. You do not yet know how I manage my theater. I will visit Joseph Bouquet, and I will tell him how you pled for my mercy on his behalf."

"Angel." When he doesn't reply, I call again.

But he is gone. So after waiting a while, I take off the garters and corset, put on my nightdress, and go to sleep.

9

JOSEPH

My eyes blink open. Blearily I try to make sense of my location, my position. Water is sloshing somewhere near me, and there's a haze of candle-glow in the murky gloom. I can smell wet metal and damp rock—and the thick, cloying fragrance of roses.

I am naked, tied to the gate of the canal that runs beside Erik's subterranean lair. My arms and legs are stretched wide, bound with a careful series of beautiful braidlike knots. *Shibari*, Erik calls it. A technique of sexual bondage he learned from a book and adapted to suit his own style. My muscles and my flesh bulge between the neat crisscrossing sections of rope. My balls are circled by a loop of rope, and my cock hangs limp through a gap in the bindings. There's a rope traveling between my butt cheeks, grazing my asshole.

My stomach surges with nausea. "Bastard," I gasp. "You drugged me while I was asleep and brought me down here. I have work, you know. I can't play with you today."

"Oh, but you can." Erik emerges from the shadows, dressed in a neat black suit complete with a fine tailcoat. He holds a short knife, testing the point with his finger. "I sent a note to your overseer. You have the day off. So you and I can—play."

In the six years I've known him, I have learned all of Erik's moods. The half of his face that's uncovered by the mask is pale as stone, utterly icy. There's a muscle flicking in his cheek, near his jawline, and a vein is prominent along his temple.

He's truly dangerous right now.

I swallow "Is this about Christine?"

"Damn right it's about Christine," he hisses. "You tasted the inside of her mouth before I could. You thief. You son of a whore. The only reason you're not bleeding now is because Christine begged me to be kind to you." He moves closer, circling one of my nipples with his fingernail. "So I've trussed you up prettily, and here you'll stay for as long as I see fit."

"Erik," I begin, but he presses the flat of the knife blade across my lips.

"Don't beg," he says. "That comes later. You've seen me punish Matthieu before—rather often, in fact. I think he craves the attention and does naughty things on purpose, to provoke me. But that's beside the point. Now it's your turn for punishment. Accept it with grace, and I will be merciful."

He lowers the knife blade, trailing it gently under my jaw, along the slant of my throat, down my body, bumping it over the ropes. Then he tucks the tip delicately under my flaccid cock and strokes along the underside, lightly.

Breath leaks through my clenched teeth as my cock stiffens involuntarily.

"Look at that." Erik smiles. "Someone is ready to play, after all."

"Fuck you," I whisper. It's a curse and a plea, because I do want this. I always want him. Impossible to resist his masterful, magnetic presence, his goddamn beautiful voice, light and soft when he's flirting, with just enough gravel in it when he's commanding us.

Erik takes my jaw in his hand. He's slightly taller than me, with broader shoulders, though I'm burlier, more heavily muscled.

He takes my lower lip between his teeth and tugs it until it hurts a little. Then he lets it snap back into place and lashes across my lips with his wet tongue. "Fuck you?" he says softly. "I might be persuaded. But it won't be gentle."

With Matthieu or I disappoint him, Erik's anger vacillates between raging lust and sensual violence. We know—or hope—that he would stop the punishment if we asked—but neither of us have ever asked. Every time one of us infuriates him, he takes that man across a new line, into some new dimension of pleasure, often linked to pain.

Inhaling deeply to calm my churning gut, I relax in my bonds. No use resisting him even if I wanted to. "Punish me."

He flashes me the most beautiful, wicked smile I've ever seen, and my belly thrills.

And then the pain begins.

Five hours later, I'm bleeding from several tiny, precise cuts along my pectoral where Erik carved his name into my flesh. My balls ache. A couple hours ago he massaged my lower belly until I pissed onto the stones by the canal. My cock is painfully hard— Erik hasn't allowed it any rest for what feels like an eternity.

All this for one damn kiss.

But I understand why Matthieu goes through similar torment on purpose, over and over. It feels good to have Erik's sole attention focused on me— no thoughts of anyone else in his head.

"Do you repent, Joseph?" Erik asks, thumbing my nipple. He puts his mouth over it and sucks enthusiastically before biting the bud of flesh. I shout, my cock dancing, my balls tightening.

"I repent," I gasp. "I should not have kissed Christine. I only did it to test her and see if she was really a virgin, but I should have left her for you, until you were ready to share. I'm sorry. Forgive me."

I could have said it earlier. But there is an addictive magic in these games of his, one that a masochistic part of me wanted to enjoy to the fullest.

"And there we have it," purrs Erik. "I'm not going to fuck you today, Joseph. You don't deserve such a reward. But I will do this."

He circles my cock with his hand and rubs swiftly, applying pressure with his thumb, shifting his fingers expertly. I come with a hoarse scream. The pleasure is so intense I think I might break apart—my body convulses in the ropes, every muscle contorted, rock hard. Cum jets out of me, shooting far across the stone walkway. A few drops even make it to the canal.

Shaking, gasping with relief, I sag against the ropes.

Erik soothes me with his hand, then licks the tip of my cock clean.

He slices the ropes deftly in a few key spots, and the whole mass of them collapse away from my body. Then he helps me to the more civilized part of the lair, where the couches are.

I relax into a deep cushioned sofa, drawing a blanket over my body. The punishment is over. Now he will bring me food and drink, and we will sit together and talk of art, music, cooking and magic.

It's my favorite part of a session with Erik. The comfort after the pain.

"Five hours with Erik?" Matthieu gapes at me. "And then recovery time?" His eyes narrow. "I'm so fucking jealous, Joseph. I shall have to do something naughty to get his attention now."

I chuckle, knotting a rope into place. "Here's your chance." I nod to an approaching figure, wending her way toward us through the maze of props, crates, and set pieces backstage.

Christine is dressed in white—Erik made sure that I stocked the wardrobe of her new room with virginal attire, probably to ensure that Matthieu and I remember she's off limits. Her brown curls tumble around her face and the creamy curves of her exposed shoulders. Perhaps if Erik really wants us to stay away, he should have dressed her in a high-collared, floor-length dress of thick, ugly fabric. Not that such clothing would detract from the eager sweetness of her personality, which shines through her bright smile upon Matthieu and me.

"You two are friends then." She looks like a satisfied cat who has just snared a mouse. "I thought so. And you both know *him*, too, don't you?"

She's putting it all together much faster than I expected. I glance at Matthieu, unsure what to say.

Fortunately we're both prevented from answering by an outburst of strident voices and a whirl of bustling activity near one of the backstage entrances. The two new managers, Moncharmin and Richard, are making their way through the area, pointing out lighting mechanisms and costumes to the slim, elegant young gentleman who follows them.

He's taller than Matthieu, slightly shorter than me, dressed in a finely embroidered vest and a velvet tailcoat cut in the latest style—which I only know from overhearing an argument about fashion between Piangi and Carlotta two weeks ago.

Voluminous ruffles spill from the young man's collar and cuffs, and he's wearing a jeweled watch-chain. His glossy auburn hair is tied neatly back with a black bow, and his vivid blue eyes are rimmed with inky lashes. His face is delicate, almost feminine in its structure.

"Is he prettier than me?" Matthieu hisses to Christine; but she's staring at the newcomer with a look of delighted shock.

"It's Raoul," she whispers.

"Raoul?" I shoot a look of apprehension at Matt. Does Christine know this young lord? Is there a connection between them? If so, Erik will not be pleased.

"Raoul and I are friends," she says. "He came to my school on a number of occasions, and we spent time together. We read a book of dark fairytales, had a picnic by the pond, promenaded in the gardens— he's a lovely person."

"Did you have a romantic inclination to this 'lovely person'?" Matthieu asks.

"Oh no," she says, pink suffusing her cheeks. "We were thirteen or so. Completely innocent. Good friends, is all. *Mon dieu,* he has grown up well. Rather handsome, isn't he? I don't suppose he would recognize or remember me, though."

Matthieu stares at me desperately, but I cannot think what to do or say. Christine's eyes track the managers and the young lord. Apparently she has forgotten all about us.

"May we have your attention, please!" Moncharmin bellows suddenly to everyone backstage. Dancers pause halfway through tying on their shoes, lamplighters lean down from the catwalk overhead, and scene handlers turn around to listen. Madame Giry is there as well, flanked by the other dance instructors, and the maestro stands nearby, sweating as usual, gripping a stack of sheet music.

"This young gentleman is our new patron, Raoul, Vicomte de Chagny. He wanted to view the theater and meet everyone before the performance tomorrow night."

The Vicomte waves genially, smiling. "I honor the work you do here." His voice is pleasant, his diction cultured and crisp. "The arts are so important to the good health of a nation. You are blessing new generations with the riches of beauty, music, and performance. Best wishes to you all, and I look forward to seeing the production tomorrow."

It's a good speech, and it sounds genuine. The Vicomte continues to move ahead, clasping hands with everyone from the grimy errand boy to the maestro himself.

The managers make no effort to introduce him to Christine as the new leading lady. Perhaps they did not tell him that Carlotta has left, fearing that he might remove his donation. The Vicomte passes on, moving away from our corner, continuing his tour through the Opera House in the company of the managers.

Christine looks deeply disappointed, but there's no time for her to speak of it further, because the seamstress comes to hustle her away for more costume adjustments.

"I thought he was rather insolent," says Matthieu. "A cocky brat of a noble. Eh, Joseph?"

"He's very attractive," I say. "And he's generous, rich, and well-spoken. The type of man a girl like Christine would be lucky to have."

Matthieu nods disconsolately. "We should tell Erik."

"*You* should tell Erik. I have work to do."

"Tell Erik what?" murmurs a voice behind us.

We both whirl, startled. And there he is, a looming figure barely visible in the shadow of a great wooden stag, one of the set pieces for Act One. Half of his handsome face is bare, while the other is concealed beneath his usual white mask. His sleek black hair is perfectly groomed, except for one roguish curl that bounces against his brow. His cruel, beautiful mouth hitches in a half-smile when he sees how shocked we are.

"Boys," he says softly. "What do you need to tell me?"

I snort. Boys, indeed. At twenty-six, he is only four years my senior, and six years older than Matt.

Matthieu is already chattering in a low tone, explaining to Erik about Raoul and Christine.

A muscle along Erik's jaw pulses. "And this young lord will be attending the opera tomorrow night?"

"Yes," Matthieu replies.

"He will see Christine, and he will recognize her, because she is not someone a man could ever forget," Erik muses. "He will want to claim her and court her. He'll come to her dressing room afterward to give her flowers, as admirers do. We must be ready. Joseph, tomorrow night, after the performance, you will allow her no visitors except the managers. You'll escort Christine back to her bedroom immediately after they leave, and I'll take care of the rest. As for you, Matthieu—"

"I'll be your patient little dancing puppet on the sidelines, I know," Matt sighs.

"Actually, I have a delicious job for you. We must lure Christine deeper into the joys of the flesh, addict her to us so she will have no thoughts left for the polite, chaste company of the Vicomte." Erik's teeth flash in a savage smile. "Tonight, Matthieu, you will eat her pussy so well she will be ruined for another man's tongue. And then tomorrow night, I will fuck her. It's sooner than I planned, but if you do

91

your duty well, I have no doubt she will be desperate for my cock after her performance."

"So when I kissed her, I was punished, and now Matt gets to lick her?" I growl in an undertone. "How is that fair?"

"Plans change," Erik says. "To make it up to you, on the night that we share her, you may take her pussy first. Or second. Whatever you prefer."

An image rises in my mind—Christine naked on her back, legs wide, watching us take turns with her, her sex sloppy with our shared cum.

I swallow hard as my cock stiffens. "You have a deal."

10

CHRISTINE

Once again, I can't sleep.

There's been no song from the Angel, and I miss him. I miss the clear beauty of his voice singing to me, the patient instruction he offers for my music. When I'm with him I am thoroughly awake and alive, every bit of me. I sing for him better than I sing for anyone else. And in his presence I feel the constant tantalizing heat of things unspoken—filthy, delightful secrets we can share.

I pace my room, aching to walk the halls but afraid that if I leave, I won't hear it if the Angel finally does speak to me. Surely he will come to me tonight. Tomorrow is my first big performance—me, a girl who has barely just arrived here. It's too strange, too impossible. I can hardly believe it is happening.

I know the other chorus girls resent me, despite the fact that my voice is objectively the best at the Opera aside from Carlotta's. Perhaps, for those who prefer a smoother tone and less flamboyance, I am even better than Carlotta.

Or perhaps I am growing too vain and proud. The headmistress at Marchette used to warn us of vanity and pride. We were never to praise our own talents; we must wait for others to do so, and when they did, we must turn the compliments aside with humble phrases, passing the honor on to others. We were never to express superiority over anyone else, by word, deed, or look. We were to smile placidly and speak calmly.

But a fire has woken in me since I arrived—since I had my first orgasm and made sounds I've never been allowed to make. I can feel the cracks branching through the foundation of what I've been taught. I suspect it would take one well-placed blow to shatter it all and set me free—if freedom is truly what I want.

What is it that I want? And is freedom always this terrifying?

I pace the room twice more, end to end, and call out, "Angel?" with no answer.

And then someone raps on my door.

I startle, suddenly conscious that I'm wearing only my panties and corset. Quickly I sweep a lacy, gauzy robe around myself—it doesn't provide much coverage, but it's the only one I've been given.

When I open the door, Matthieu is standing there, naked from the waist up—which isn't unusual, since he's shirtless in every scene of the Opera. He plays a slave boy, along with five other male dancers. "A pleasure slave," he told me once, with a wink. But somehow, seeing him shirtless onstage and being this close to his warm, bare skin at night are two very different things.

He's still wearing the gold paint from rehearsal on his lips, cheeks, and eyelids. His long lashes sparkle with it. He mouths the ring in his lower lip and gazes at me, a sultry heaviness in his eyes.

"Christine," he says, and my name has never sounded more beautiful.

"Do you need something?" I ask. "I'm—waiting for—" I glance backward over my shoulder as if the Angel might suddenly materialize.

"He is pleased with you," Matthieu says softly.

"Who?" I gasp. "You mean—"

He nods. His lashes dip even lower, and the tip of his tongue glides over his lip. "The Angel. He wants to encourage you for tomorrow's performance. He sent me with a reward for you."

"Is it cock?" I whisper, my pulse skittering.

A grin spreads over Matthieu's face. "No, *ma petite chatte*, it isn't my cock. But it's the next best thing."

I should say no. The fear of men has been hammered into my head since my father's death. Stay away from them, don't speak to them any more than necessary, don't open your heart to them, don't let them touch you. They will hurt you, every time. Our headmistress was very clear on that point, and I could hear the pain of past wrongs in her voice whenever she said it. I believed her, because the important man in my life, my father, left me. He died, and I was taken from our home full of music and beautiful things, to be placed in the confines of the Marchette School.

Men will hurt you, every time.

But this man, barely more than a boy, is smiling at me with such openness in his handsome face, such real affection in his green eyes. He likes me, truly. He wants to do naughty things to me, as a reward from my Angel. And I want to let him in.

I move back, allowing him to enter my room. When he does, I close the door carefully. "No one saw you?"

"No. The Angel had you placed here so you'd be away from others who might interfere with his plans."

A trickle of caution runs through my joy. "That sounds a little ominous."

"He intends you no harm, Christine. None of us do. We never could. You are a treasure, a queen. We only want to worship you."

"We?" I swallow, touching my chest nervously. "You and Joseph and the Angel, you are somehow in this together? Who are you to each other? And what is all of this?"

"The Angel will explain when it is time," Matthieu says. "For now, know that our highest purpose is your success, your freedom, and your pleasure. We are all devoted to it."

Naïve I may be, but I am not a complete fool. There is more to this than he's revealing, and I suspect a darker motive behind it. But I reassure myself that when the truth finally comes out, I will have a choice. Matthieu says they honor my freedom, which is more than people have done for me my entire life. Never has anyone claimed that his highest purpose was my success and pleasure. My heart thumps harder, just from the echo of those words in my mind.

"What is this reward you were sent to give?" I ask.

"An offer of worship," Matthieu says. "If you will lie on the bed, I will do everything else."

My pulse is pounding in my throat, throbbing between my legs. I can feel my clit swelling, a sharp tingle running through it over and over. I drop my robe.

When I recline on the bed, Matthieu drapes himself at the end of it, near the mirror. He begins by lifting my foot and kissing the hollow of my ankle. At the first tender press of his soft lips, I shiver and claw fistfuls of the blanket.

He smiles gently against my skin and kisses a little higher—the curve of my calf. A little higher, to my shin, then my knee. He's moving upward, his beautiful lithe body shifting languidly between my parted legs, his fingers gliding lazily along my skin.

I cannot believe I am allowing this. I am letting a man touch me intimately. In a moment he will be looking at my naked sex.

Every press of his fingers is a tiny explosion of hot pleasure.

Another kiss, on the inside of my leg right above the knee. Matthieu sweeps a warm palm along my inner thigh, grazing upward while my sex quivers in anticipation.

His fingertips find the waistband of my panties and he draws them down along my legs, altering his position until he can take them off and toss them aside. Then he's back again, his mouth close to my center. Like the other dancers, I shave my whole body regularly, and after my bath tonight I'm smooth and fragrant, which he seems to like. His pupils are dilated, his lips parted as he admires me.

"Your pussy is so pink. These lips—thick and delicious, perfect for nibbling. And this inner part— like the ruffled petals of a rose." He's moving my folds aside as he speaks, with a delicate touch that makes me whimper. "Look at the inside of you, Christine. Look at this perfect little hole." He strokes along the inside of my pussy, probing gently. "You're so wet, sweetheart. I'm going to taste these sweet juices now. May I?"

I think I have forgotten to breathe while he was examining me. I inhale quickly and gasp, "Yes."

"Mmm." He hums in response, and his tongue sweeps through me, over me. A sharp, clear note of ecstasy breaks from my throat, and I arch back on the pillows.

I'm already liquid with desire, but when Matthieu's gold lip ring grazes my clit, I ignite. "God, god, god, Matthieu!" I pant, and he smiles against my pussy, green eyes flicking up to mine as he keeps licking me. The sight of his golden head between my legs, his bare torso flexing, his ringed hands bracing my thighs—it's almost too much. Ripples, waves, oceans of pleasure are flowing through my entire body.

This is heaven, and there is an angel suckling my clit.

He takes one of my pussy lips in his teeth, oh so gently, nibbles it, and bathes it all over with his tongue. He nuzzles across my slit with another affectionate lick, and mouths the other side of my pussy before returning to the tiny pulsing bud at the top. He laps it, faster and faster, until I'm writhing, tearing at the blankets, shrilling notes of pure pleasure. My belly heaves, aching, surging as the bliss mounts higher inside me, peaking to a crescendo.

Matthieu sets his lip ring against the tip of my clit and bobs his head, swirling the glossy bit of gold round and round.

Ecstasy explodes through my body, a lightning-crack along my spine, glory infusing every nerve. I arch off the bed, but Matthieu braces me with steady hands, kissing my pussy deeply, drinking my orgasm.

When I finally go limp on the bed, he sits up and massages my pussy gently with his hand, slower and slower as I come down from the height. I'm panting, my eyes drifting closed, my thighs trembling.

With a final pat to my pussy, Matthieu rises from the bed, his jaw tight and his eyes burning with desperation. His pants are bulging oddly.

He goes into the privy, leaving the door half-open.

I'm still shaky, but I'm also curious what he's doing in there. Washing his face, maybe?

I swing my legs off the bed and wobble over to the doorway, leaning forward until I can peer inside.

And what I see takes my breath away.

Matthieu has unfastened his pants, and his cock protrudes from them. It's longer than my hand, about three or four fingers thick—much bigger than the male organs I've seen on statues and in sketches. And instead of hanging down, soft and floppy, it juts out in front of him, curving slightly upward.

The head of his cock is arrow-shaped, but fatter, and there is a tiny slit at the tip, where a bit of liquid is seeping out.

Matthieu doesn't notice me. His back is angled toward the door, while I'm leaning in far enough to see past the line of his body.

His cock looks strange, but it's oddly attractive, too. The sight of it heats my blood all over again and sends a prickle of awareness to my exposed clit. Is it possible to have a second orgasm so soon after the first?

Tentatively I press my fingers over my naughty clit to still it. And then I massage it, very slightly, as I watch Matthieu wrap his hand around the long shaft between his legs.

He moans, then bites his wrist to quiet himself. His hand pumps along his length, stopping just beneath his cock head. "Fuck," he says softly, and then he spreads a hand over his own breast, fondling the flesh, squeezing the nipple.

Suddenly I want to be a part of this. I want to be pressed against his back, my skin against his. I want to show him that I care, that I'm grateful for his kindness since the day I arrived. I want to show him how much I enjoyed his mouth on me.

My heart thunders in my chest as I creep closer and press myself to his back. My cheek rests against his shoulder, and my hair glides against his bare skin.

He tenses, sucking in a quick breath. "Christine…"

I slide my arms beneath his, circling his body from behind, cupping his pectorals. He takes my wrists in both his hands as if he's going to make me stop touching him—but he doesn't. He stands perfectly still, with me latched around him, the bare mound of my pussy pressed to his firm ass.

I roll the tiny buds of his nipples between my fingers, like I saw him doing to himself. A harsh groan shakes his body, and when I peep over his shoulder at his cock, it's bouncing, naked and untouched.

It needs to be touched.

My right hand slides down his chest, flowing over the planes of his toned stomach, down to the base of his penis.

"He's going to kill me for this," whispers Matthieu. I know he means the Angel.

"He won't," I whisper back, and I circle his cock with my fingers, dragging them along his length. "Like this?"

"Fuck," he moans. "Like that."

With my left hand still clasped over his breast and my body melded to his, I work my hand along his shaft. It's so hot and smooth; I can't help running my fingers along the veins of it, touching the sticky liquid at the tip.

"What is going to happen?" I whisper.

"If you keep stroking my cock," he breathes raggedly. "I'm going to ejaculate. My cum will spurt out, and it will make me feel wonderful, like you felt."

"I want to see your cock spurt cum," I say quietly. "I like the way it feels in my hand. So big and hard, but your skin is soft. I love your cock. I love your ass, too. When I rub against it, I feel as if I might come again." My hips surge against his bottom. I keep speaking, hardly knowing what I'm saying—letting every thought and feeling pour out of me into his ear. "Matthieu, I want to know how your beautiful cock would feel slipping inside me."

"Fuck me," he whimpers, shaking in my arms. "Faster, please god."

I stroke him faster, a clumsy rhythm at first, but then I find a motion that takes him from low whimpering to a shrill, needy whine. His whole body tightens, hardens—his cock throbs, and white fluid pumps out of it, dripping onto the floor. He sounds as if he's crying.

"Did I hurt you?" I ask.

"No. Fuck, that felt so good." He shudders all over. "Christine, you were made for sex and song. You are naturally gifted at both. The words you spoke to me—that was the most aroused I've been in a long time."

"So I did well?" A smile spreads over my face as he turns around and pulls me into his arms.

"You did so well," he murmurs against my forehead. "Such a good girl."

"Can you make me come again before you leave?" I ask. "Is that possible?"

"Oh Christine." He laughs. "That is possible, and much more."

He takes me to the bed and this time he lies beside me, propped on one elbow while his hand expertly tantalizes my pussy. His fingers work me nearly to the peak, and then he crawls between my legs and slips his hands under my bottom, lifting me while he leans down. He makes me come against his mouth while his hands knead my bare ass cheeks.

When he lowers me back into the blankets, I am utterly spent. My body is flushed, heaving, singing with the echoes of the orgasm. I'm still wearing the corset, and I notice Matthieu eyeing my breasts longingly as he prepares to leave.

"Do you want to see them?" I ask.

"Not tonight," he says. "I've already pushed Erik's good graces far enough." And then he claps a hand over his mouth.

I sit bolt upright. "Erik? That's the Angel's name?"

"Yes." Matthieu grimaces. "You've completely undone me, Christine. I don't usually let secrets slip."

"It's all right," I say. "All of this is fine, because he sent you here." Suddenly uncertain, I frown. "You did want to do this, *oui*? You didn't pleasure me only because he ordered it? I would hate to think he forced you—"

"Of course not!" He darts back to me, tips my face up, and kisses my forehead. "I've wanted this since the day I saw you on the steps of the Opera House. I'd have had you sooner, but I needed to wait for his blessing."

"What is he to you, that you need his blessing?"

Matthieu sighs. "He is leader, lover, friend, and more. You will understand when the time is right, sweetheart. And now I must go. I will see you tomorrow, my cherished diva, for your Opening Night."

And with an airy kiss of his fingers to me, he leaves the room.

11

RAOUL

I arrive late to the opera. It's a bad habit of mine, always being late to things. One of the many reasons I was kicked out of multiple schools throughout my education.

I'm not usually the type to visit the opera—I prefer a merry gathering at the racetracks with good friends, plenty of drink, and a little of the fragrant weed my friends like to smoke. Though lately my friends have been more absorbed with smoking, betting, drinking, fucking, and playing juvenile pranks than anything else.

They seem to have forgotten that we once dreamed of doing important things when we became adults. Now that the time has arrived, they're content to roll along, spending our parents' money hand over fist.

There's a restless itch inside me, a burning to do something useful, something *important* with my money. My parents had me when they were middle-aged, and they're failing quickly now, soon to pass on into the next life. The vast inheritance, the influence, and the title are mine, to do with as I see fit. And I think I see fit to do *good*, somewhere, somehow. I will not drink myself into a stupor at the racetrack or in the salons every day. I refuse to rut with any buxom barmaid or racetrack floozy who will bend over and hike up her skirts for me. That's how my friend Charles behaves. He's got three or four illegitimate children already—children he refuses to care for financially.

I will not be like him. I have had a romantic interlude or two, nothing serious. One day I will marry properly, and bed only my spouse, and have legitimate children like a respectable gentleman of rank.

In the meantime, I am supporting the Opera House, and indulging in my passion for beautiful horses. I keep a very fine stable. Two of my loveliest mares are with me tonight, pulling my private carriage. I leap out, trusting my man Yves to see the horses to the Opera House stables while I run inside.

Perhaps it is not fitting for a man of my station to race up the steps of L'Opera Lajeunesse, but I do it anyway. The activity gets my heart pumping, brings blood to my cheeks. I feel invigorated. How long has it been since I engaged in any vigorous activity except riding?

In the soft light from the chandeliers, the lobby of the Opera House looks beautiful, dreamlike. I breeze past a footman who recognizes me and reaches for my cloak, with a respectful, "Vicomte," and a quick bow. I toss my cloak to him, along with my hat. When he sees I'm not going to stop, he points up some stairs and calls out a box number, which I don't quite hear because a door opens somewhere and a blast of orchestral music washes out into the lobby.

It is no matter. Messieurs Richard and Moncharmin pointed in the direction of my box when I came by to tour the theater. I think I can find it.

Box 5, I believe it was.

I hurry along the hushed upper hallway, the tromp of my boots muffled by thick crimson carpet. Ah, here it is. Box 5, inscribed in gilt letters on a plaque of gleaming wood. I slip through the door into the gloomy shadow of the curtained box.

Odd that there is not so much as a candle here, and no tray of champagne and sweets for the patron of the theater. No matter. I am not a difficult man to please. I can easily view the opera without anything to eat, though I would not have minded a drink.

There are two rows of deep, cushioned chairs, their armrests padded for comfort. I bump against one, cursing under my breath. So infernally dark up here. It is a good thing the railing is high, or I might tumble over it and break my neck upon some unsuspecting guests below.

I fumble my way into a seat, my eyes on the stage. Some half-dressed men are dancing about. Very attractive men. I've always noticed the bodies and charms of both men and women, though my parents remain resolved that I will marry a nice girl, preferably a titled one, and I am inclined to agree, for the sake of fathering progeny. When my parents are gone, with my relatives few and far away, I'll be left alone to carry on the family name.

More lights flare up on the stage, and by their distant glow I glance around at my box again, surveying the seats, the ornate banister, the rich curtains with their heavy fringe. I notice a small table set between two of the chairs in the row behind me, with a silver tray bearing a crystal bottle of liquor and a single glass, already partly full.

So the managers did not forget me, after all.

Gratefully I reach back and take the drink. I swallow a sip at once, humming with pleasure as the whiskey warms my throat.

"Single-grain, seventy years old, aged in a sherry cask of Spanish oak," says a melodic male voice from somewhere behind me.

I startle and spill the drink on my lap. "Goddamn it!"

"Savory, darkly sugared, earthy notes," continues the voice. "I paid well for it, and I had planned to enjoy it alone on this most illustrious of opening nights."

"My apologies," I gasp, half-rising and placing the glass back on the silver tray. "I did not know—I must have entered the wrong box. Forgive me. I am a patron here, you see, but new to the theater, and I thought—"

"The Vicomte Raoul de Chagny?" The voice carries a keen note of interest.

"Yes! Yes, that is me. Or I. Or—sorry, I shall leave at once."

"Stay." A figure shifts in the shadowed recesses of the box, in the farthest seat from mine. The man appears to be cloaked, and part of his face might be bandaged. I cannot quite make it out. But if he is disfigured or injured, I will only make matters worse by staring, so I turn back around.

"So sorry, again," I say.

Someone from another box hisses, "Hush!" so I fall silent. Because of the angle and shape of the walls, I cannot see into any of the other boxes, nor can they see me. No one from below can see into Box 5 either, and the lights of the stage would prevent the dancers' and singers' eyes from piercing the darkness. Complete and utter privacy—that is what Box 5 offers. Perhaps that is why this gentleman has chosen it.

"You must be very uncomfortable, with that wet spot on your trousers," says the cloaked man. "I have a handkerchief here. You are welcome to use it."

"Oh, thank you." I turn in my seat, reaching back.

But he does not lean forward to hand it to me. "Come here, Vicomte."

He sounds younger than I at first thought. And there is something dark and insolent in the way he speaks my title. As if he resents it, or thinks it humorous.

Of course, I did barge into his box and drink his expensive aged whiskey. So he is right to be a little peeved with me.

I rise with a half-bow and step around my row of seats into his. Yes, he is cloaked, and hooded too. There's a pale flash of unnatural white beneath the hood.

"How old are you?" he asks.

"I just turned twenty."

"So young, and already so rich and powerful. Titled, and trusted because of the title. Able to hold a seat at the table, and to influence governing bodies. Able to suggest change, and then enforce it. You have power and privilege. And you want to use it well, don't you? You wish to have some beneficial impact on this world, beyond what your peers can manage."

"I suppose." Why is my heart beating so fast? It is some combination of his mesmerizing voice and his words—so similar to the words I have spoken to myself in the night, when I ache to make a difference, to heal some of the wounds of the world. How does this man already understand me, when I have exchanged so few words with him?

"Closer, Vicomte." The order is delivered with the gentle croon of a lullaby. I take another step toward him—within arm's reach now.

His hand emerges from the cloak, holding the handkerchief. He presses it to the front of my pants,

111

rubbing lightly. The fabric skims my cock, wakening the nerves.

I jump back. "I'll do it myself, thank you."

"As you like."

I snatch the handkerchief and return to my seat, thoroughly rattled. I begin dabbing at the whiskey stain, but I'm distressed to find my dick half-hard. Trying to mop up the wetness only makes me harder.

And then, just as I am at the height of my discomfort, a familiar voice begins to sing.

At the first notes, I seize the opera glasses from their little pouch beneath the banister and peer at the stage.

I'm not imagining things. It really is Christine, clad in a gown of silver, with glittering stars in her hair. I would know her voice and manner anywhere.

This girl was my friend, years ago, when our schools used to join for the occasional promenade or festivity. During the few visits we spent together, she charmed me completely. She was also the object of most of my wet dreams as a fourteen and fifteen-year-old boy. I tried to stop dreaming of her, but I could not help it. She still appears in my fantasies at times, older in my mind's eye, but as sweet, genuine, and lovely as ever. Strange how closely my mental image of her adult self matches the reality.

Her graceful neck and shoulders emerge from a cloud of silvery tulle, and in the glow of the stage lights she appears utterly angelic. Entirely desirable.

I heard her sing twice at the Marchette School for Girls, when my class was visiting there. Her voice was always remarkable, but she has improved dramatically. Her voice lilts easily through a run, soars strong and smooth for several bars, then dips low, skipping from note to note, perfectly on-pitch, at least as far as my untrained ears can tell. The end of her aria draws a dramatic roar of applause from the audience.

Tossing the opera glasses onto the seat beside me, I leap to my feet, clapping and whistling between two fingers. When the shouts and clapping die down, I resume my seat.

"Christine," I murmur. "No one told me she was the star of the show."

"Miss Christine Daaé," murmurs my hooded friend. "She took to the stage after the former prima donna left in a great uproar over ghosts or some such nonsense. I am surprised you didn't hear of the scandal among your noble friends."

"My friends are not interested in the arts," I say.

"More's the pity. But you are?"

"I am. I was. I mean, I would like to be. I'm very interested in horses. But I've always enjoyed music, too, though I've rarely visited the opera or the ballet. In fact, hearing Christine sing years ago is what first awakened a stronger interest in the performing arts. But I was not in a position to indulge that liking until recently."

"And now you wish to prove yourself as a mature and polished gentleman, by serving as patron to this lovely establishment." The sarcastic twist to his tone is unmistakable.

"Something like that," I reply. There are wooden dragons being pushed across the stage now, accompanied by marching soldiers. Not of much interest to me, so I half-turn to look at my companion. "You seem to resent me, sir, beyond my invasion of your box and my waste of your whiskey."

He's quiet for a moment. "I do resent you, yes. I see your pretty face, your fine body, your wealth and your privilege. I see in you everything I wish I could have."

My face heats and I turn back toward the stage. "I cannot change who I am, or give you what I have."

"Perhaps you could," he croons. "You could give me everything you have, Vicomte. And you *will* give me all I ask of you."

I'm sweating under the layers of my fine clothes, yearning to strip them off, to run, to leap into a cold lake or do something very, very brave and important. When he says nothing else, I glance over my shoulder.

He is gone.

What a strange man.

I try to keep my mind on the opera, which seems to be telling a tale of dragons raping maidens and men fucking dragons for magic. It's all very shocking. I already know about the War of Dragons—what schoolboy does not? But this opera's intent seems to

114

be to paint everything in the most lurid colors possible.

I have always wondered if the war was quite justified. Destroying an entire race of sentient beings like the dragons was perhaps going a bit far, despite their crimes and those of the mages.

Before the end of Act One, the managers of the Opera House bustle into Box 5. "Monsieur le Vicomte! We have found you! You are not meant to be here, *non, mais non.* We have a fine place for you in Box 2. Please, come with us."

They usher me out, and I do not protest. I'm glad to leave the dark, shrouded space and its mysterious occupant behind.

As we move into the hallway, Moncharmin whispers to Richard, "Did you leave that money in this box, as the note demanded?"

"Of course not," replies Richard. "Did you?"

"Of course not. Why should I listen to a ghost's demands?"

And they laugh together, a little too loudly.

"A ghost?" I ask, as they hurry me along to Box 2.

"The Phantom of the Opera," says Moncharmin, in a tone dripping with disbelief. "A prankster, nothing more. He sent a note demanding money, asking for Box 5 to be kept open for his sole use. Of course we did not concede to his demands. Though no one would buy tickets for Box 5." Moncharmin glances at his partner. "Odd, isn't it?"

115

"But there *was* a guest in Box 5," I say. "A strange gentleman in a cloak, with a hood, and his face was…" But my voice trails off as the two managers stare at me in horror.

"A guest? In Box 5? Impossible. None of those seats were sold."

"Perhaps there was some clerical error?" I suggest.

"No, no. But never mind that now, Vicomte, come along," says Richard, desperately cheerful. "Let us eat, yes? And let us drink to this night of triumph!"

The trays they have set out in Box 2 exceed my expectations. Chocolates, tiny flaky pastries with berries and sugar, delicately wrapped seafood on ice, miniature sandwiches. I eat, and I drink deeply of the delicious wine they offer. Soon my memory of the unsettling encounter in Box 5 begins to fade, and I think only of Christine, who shines throughout each act of the opera. There is only a tiny wobble on one note, two lines which have to be prompted, and a slight misstep in the choreography. But she handles every incident with perfect grace, smiling and moving on.

"By all accounts, it's a more seamless performance than La Carlotta ever offered," says Moncharmin, swaying slightly in his seat. His nose is much pinker than it was earlier.

Gently I remove the wine glass from his reach. "I should like to pay a visit to your prima donna after the performance, if I may."

"Of course, lad—I mean, Vicomte—our cherished patron—of course!" He hiccups and plucks a bit of shrimp from its bed of lettuce. "Anything you want. We can perhaps—hic—introduce you."

"I already know the lady." I bow my head in gracious acknowledgement of his offer. "But thank you."

I gesture to one of the footmen and ask that a large bouquet be sent to Miss Daaé's dressing room, with my card. He nods, thanking me for the generous tip I include with the money, and then he leaves.

When the opera ends, I cheer and clap until my voice is hoarse and my palms sting. Then I hurry downstairs, guided by a footman, and make my way to Christine's dressing room.

A burly young man stands before it. His sleeves are rolled halfway up, sinewy brown arms crossed over his bulky chest. Is he some sort of bodyguard for the young prima donna?

"I would like to see Miss Daaé," I tell him, smiling.

"You're the Vicomte chap." He looks me up and down. For the second time tonight, I feel as if I am being assessed and found lacking.

"I'm an old friend of hers," I say. "And yes, I am also the patron of this theater."

"I was told to let no one in," replies the man, leaning toward me confidentially. "But I think you would be good for her. Better than—well—*better.*"

I eye him cautiously. "Thank you?"

"*De rien*, Vicomte." He scans me again, this time with a hint of warmth and admiration in his gaze. "A fine figure you are, sir."

"As are you." Damn. Why did I say that?

He laughs and moves aside, pushing open the door for me. As I pass him, I catch a whiff of savory scent wafting from his skin, mingled with the sharp acridity of male sweat. Something about that smell makes my senses stutter, and I forget, for a mere second, what I am doing. But then I swallow and push on, into the dressing room, reining in my thoughts to focus only on Christine.

12

CHRISTINE

I can scarcely believe my performance is over. Can barely grasp that I actually sang before an entire opera house full of people.

It was easy to pretend they weren't there, most of the time—until the applause. Even then I could imagine it away, pretend that it was just me and the Angel.

I can barely remember parts of the opera. It's all fading into a blur of exhaustion, and yet I am too rattled to change my clothes and go to bed. I sit on the stool before my dressing-room mirror, staring at my reflection.

For a moment, I imagine that behind my face is another face staring back at me—a strange one, split in two—half shadowed, half pale.

But it is my imagination, and nothing more.

Since I arrived at the Opera, I have been in a daze—too little sleep, more work than I'm used to, and then the awakening to a level of music and sensation I had no idea existed. Butterflies shiver through the space between my hips, and my heart quivers like the wings of a moth. Yet despite my inner unrest, my body is frozen in that strained space beyond exhaustion.

Here, in this moment, I see myself with horrible clarity. The naïve idiot I have been, the pleasure-crazed girl opening herself to strangers.

This is what my headmistress warned me about. The temptations of men. And like a fool, I thought I was fine because they were gentle with me, not harsh or demanding. How they must be laughing at me now—the innocent lamb, such easy prey for the wolves.

Guilt grates against my heart, and I prop my elbows on the dressing table, resting my forehead in my hands. What have I done? What am I letting myself become? A filthy woman, undeserving of the love of a proper gentleman. No one would want me if they knew how I opened myself to the Angel, how I touched Matthieu and let him lick me.

Yet even as I think of those times, my sex warms and swells. I want more. More freedom, more pleasure, more of the tantalizing wonder that each man can give me—Matthieu, Joseph, and the Angel— Erik.

Women are supposed to want only one man. God help me, I crave all three of them, each in a different way.

I am a wicked girl. There is no help for me. Perhaps I should let myself fall into the dark and dissolution, for there is no savior to pull me out of this.

Voices outside the door, and then Joseph pushes it open, making way for—

Raoul.

His bright, open smile, blue eyes, and auburn hair are the best thing I have ever seen.

"Christine," he says, and I leap from the stool and run into his arms.

Shocked breath huffs out of him, but he embraces me anyway. He's broader and taller than I remember, but he smells almost the same—mint and lavender, with a new smoky sweetness lingering on his coat.

Joseph catches my eye over Raoul's shoulder. Despite his simple clothes, he always bears himself so well, and the dip of his head in my direction is almost regal, granting me permission for this excessive display of emotion. In his warm brown eyes I read sympathy and soft pain. He closes the door, leaving Raoul and me alone.

"I am so glad to see you," I murmur into Raoul's shoulder.

"I can tell." He chuckles. "You were rarely this demonstrative at the Marchette School, Christine. Only when you and I were away from the others did I catch a glimpse of your true feelings, and even then you were so reserved. A proper lady at such a young age."

It's almost a gentle rebuke. I know he doesn't mean to hurt me, but somehow he does. I pull back, composing myself. "Did you enjoy the performance?"

"Very much so. I was wondering if you would honor me by coming to luncheon with me tomorrow."

"I have rehearsal."

"The day after?"

"I—perhaps." Some part of me is anxious about this invitation. I don't think my Angel of Music would approve. He has made it clear that he thinks of me as his.

"I will come back every night to see you," Raoul swears, his eyes sparkling. "It will be my joy to persist until you grant me this request, my lady."

He's so kind, so pleasant, so wholesome. No illicit lyrics, no suggestive words, no filthy swears. His guileless nature comforts me, even as some dark part of me wants to shock him, or possibly corrupt him.

Is that how Matthieu, Joseph, and Erik feel about me? Do they itch to infect my mind with sexual thoughts, until I see and hear sex everywhere? Because that is what they are doing, intentional or not. I find myself wondering about the length of Raoul's dick, the appearance of his nipples, how he would react if I touched him between the legs.

"Christine, you're flushed," Raoul says, frowning. He turns to the nearby table, where the water pitcher sits nearly empty. "I'll fetch you fresh water," he says, and hurries out of the room.

He has always been like that—more ready to do a task himself than to let servants take care of it. There is an inner motivation that propels him to action, and I love that about him.

I forgot how much I learned to care for him during those few visits we had together.

Joseph enters the room immediately after Raoul leaves. "Your admirer left so soon?"

His bulk seems to fill the space, a physical dominance my body can't deny. Tonight his hair isn't in locs; it's a rich halo of black curls that frame his handsome face perfectly. I can't help eyeing his broad, soft lips, wanting to taste them again. I wasn't good at kissing before. Perhaps I can do better this time.

"He went to get me some water," I tell Joseph.

"Hm." Joseph touches a glorious bouquet of roses and lilies, one of many that have been sent to my dressing room by the managers and admiring opera guests. "This one has his card. A fine bunch of blooms."

"They are beautiful." I step closer to the flowers and inhale their delicate scent. When I look up, Joseph is watching me. He looks away quickly, swallowing, and a muscle in his temple flexes.

Is he nervous around me?

The thought blazes through my system like a comet. Until now I have been focused on how *I* felt around these men—except for the incident with Matthieu, when I was attuned to his sexual sensations.

124

Touching him and making him come was a powerful experience. But perhaps I affect Joseph on a deeper level than the physical.

"You let Raoul into this room tonight," I say softly. "Why? You let no one else in."

"I think he is good for you," Joseph mutters, plucking at a rose.

"Why should you care what is good for me?"

He turns suddenly, an agony of compassion in his eyes. "Christine, you are too kind and gentle for this, for us. You must run while you have the chance. Leave with Raoul tonight, and marry him, and never come back here."

"What?" I gasp. "He hasn't asked me—he doesn't want me to marry him. *Mon Dieu*, Joseph, what are you talking about? Am I in some danger?"

"Yes."

"From Erik?"

He glances around the room apprehensively, lowering his voice. "Christine, we are all in danger. Not directly from Erik, but from his plans for us— for you. I won't lie—I want everything he has planned, selfishly, deeply." He reaches out, as if he's fighting himself, and he catches my waist. "I want you. Everything that you are. I have empty places inside me, and you fill one of those so perfectly, Christine. I have watched you. I see you. You're lonely, like I was. You have no one in the world, so when the wolves come, you are too hungry for love, and you cannot deny them."

My lips tremble, and I drop my gaze from his.

"You are letting him manipulate you," Joseph whispers. "If that is what you want, so be it. But you should know that you have power too. Erik wants to be in control, but he needs someone to remind him that he isn't a phantom or an angel, only a man. If you stay, let it be on your terms."

"And you?" I whisper. "Where is your power?"

"I have found my power in submitting to him. That is my choice. Yours can be different." He's whispering to me, his face a breath from mine, our foreheads touching.

I tilt up my mouth, brushing my lips to his.

"I can't kiss you until he allows it," he groans.

"The Angel is brilliant and demanding," I whisper. "Matthieu is sweet and insecure and funny. And you—you're a storyteller, a baker, a beautiful god of a man—" I run my fingers along his hard, muscled forearm. "You're the wise and unselfish one, aren't you?"

"Christine," he pants. "I have to kiss you."

"Raoul will be back any minute."

He closes his eyes, exhaling deeply. Then he steps away from me, his fists clenched, his face resuming its mask of control. I can see it now, how much he is like me. He wears the face he is expected to wear—contented and calm, performing his daily duties. But inside are deep, deep longings, passions that have entangled him with Erik and Matthieu, and now with me.

"Are you intimate with them?" I ask quietly. "Erik and Matthieu? Do you touch them and watch them come?"

"That and more."

"More?"

"Men have a hole too," he says simply.

My eyes widen, and he shakes his head with a rueful chuckle.

"I won't explain how it works now. Your Vicomte is bound to return in a moment, unless something has waylaid him. Something—or someone..." Joseph looks suddenly concerned. "You should return to your bedroom, Christine. I will go and check on the Vicomte and tell him you have retired for the night. It is late. He can see you tomorrow."

I know the Angel of Music—Erik—will contact me tonight. But I do not wait for him in my underthings. I put on a simple white dress and take the pins out of my hair, letting it cascade around my shoulders.

My feet are a little sore, but not nearly as sore as they would be if I'd been dancing with the girls instead of singing Carlotta's role. I sit on the edge of the bed and massage them.

"*Bravo, ma cherié.*" A melodious masculine voice echoes around my room, making goosebumps rise all over my skin. "*Tu as bien fait ce soir.*"

The praise sends a quick throb of pleasure to my clit, but I steel myself against my body's response, remembering what Joseph said. I do not have to be completely malleable in the Angel's hands. He needs me, wants me, and that gives me power.

"I'm so happy to have pleased you, Angel," I say. "I wish I could see your face, so I could thank you more... personally."

"And you will see me, little one," he purrs. "Come to the mirror."

Rising, I pad over to the huge mirror and stand before it. I look pale, as usual, but two bright patches of rosy color burn in my cheeks.

The room seems to be humming, surging—ripples flowing through the glass, mist curling from the cold metal and winding around me. Through the swirling mist, music drifts, whispering in my mind.

Dazed, I reach out, and when my fingertips touch the mirror it isn't glass at all, but a viscous liquid through which my hand passes easily.

"Come to me, darling girl," he sings softly. "Come and meet your Angel."

I hold my breath and step through the glimmering surface.

It feels like water, but when I've passed through, my clothes, skin, and hair are dry. I'm in a pitch-black space, but almost immediately candles wink to life in recesses along a corridor that stretches into the distance.

And in that hallway, several paces away from me, stands a man.

He's very tall, taller than Joseph, and his shoulders are immensely broad, though his waist is narrow, like the tapered body of a dancer or swimmer. From his shoulders hangs a heavy cloak, and the shadow of its hood conceals his face. More mist curls around him, clinging to him as if it's drawn to his presence as irresistibly as I am.

"Come," he says, extending his hand.

"Take off your hood first." I cannot believe that demand left my mouth. Apparently neither can he, because he freezes for a moment, as if he's about to rebuke me.

But then he reaches up and pushes the hood back.

He's painfully handsome. A face that is all wicked edges, bone and beauty and flashing eyes. Yet half of that sharp face is concealed by a white mask. His glossy black hair is slicked back from his forehead, but it doesn't seem to like being controlled—a curl or two have escaped to grace his temple and brow.

He cannot be much older than me. A handful of years, perhaps.

The oddest thing about him is his eyes. Both the uncovered one and the one shining through the mask are yellow, like sunflower petals, like canary feathers—bright, rich yellow.

"Now will you come with me?" he says.

The mist swirls around me, teasing my skin, and I shudder at the faint chill of it. Walking slowly forward, I look at his outstretched hand—strong and supple, decorated with heavy rings.

"You are the Phantom, the Opera Ghost, aren't you?"

"I am many things," he says, in the smooth, clear voice I've come to love so well. "Poet, composer, painter, sculptor. Architect, chemist, trickster, and magician. Above all I adore music. And you, Christine, are the perfect vessel for the music in my soul. You are the key to unlocking my innermost talent, my true nature."

I have laid my fingers in his. He's drawing me close—the scent of roses, cedar, licorice, and pepper. His unique fragrance. I am enveloped and enticed by it.

"I can't believe I am touching you at last," he says unsteadily. And it's that quiver in his voice, that wondering, incredulous gratitude, that makes me yield to him.

He turns, leading me with him, singing softly as we walk. It's one of the tunes from *La Guerre des Dragons*, and I harmonize with him to ground myself, to feel secure in all this strangeness. Our voices blend perfectly, even better now that there are no walls between us.

We descend, by stairways and passageways, and as we travel lower he seems less afraid that our duet may be heard. We sing full-voice now, adding riffs and runs wherever we like. He looks at me, his yellow eyes flashing with joy and triumph, as our voices soar together.

The stone walls have opened around us, revealing vast underground chambers bisected by a canal of rippling dark water. The acoustics in the space are oddly magnificent, and the echo gives our song an otherworldly timbre.

There's a boat floating on the canal, and Erik helps me into it. He stands behind me, poling the skiff through the water, while I keep humming.

As long as there is music between us, we do not have to talk of the strangeness of this, and I do not have to ask why he has brought me down here. If he merely wanted my body, we could have performed that act in my room. This is about sex, I'm sure, but it's also about something else, and I desperately want to know more.

At last we pass under a metal gate, which can be lowered to block the canal. Erik brings the boat up to a stony walkway. He ties it off, then climbs out and reaches down to me.

When I step out, my body bumps softly against his, chest to chest.

He reaches up to brush my cheek with his knuckles, running his fingers into my hair, cupping the nape of my neck.

"Why do you wear that mask?" I lift my fingers to touch it, but he catches my wrist.

"No," he says sharply. "You must not remove it. Promise me."

"I wanted you before I knew you had a body," I tell him. "I will still want you, no matter what scars or differences you hide."

"You may think so. But you know nothing." The edge in his tone startles me.

He catches me by the shoulders, whirls me around, and walks me toward an open area overlooking the canal. Candelabra shed golden light over couches, tasseled cushions, rich rugs, low bookcases stuffed with volumes.

To my right, on a low platform surrounded by more waist-high bookshelves, is a fine organ with gleaming, polished pipes.

Wooden partitions draped with feather boas and thin chains divide the back area of the space, and several huge framed paintings are propped against the rock wall. Between two of those paintings is an arched doorway, half-draped with veils of gauzy black fabric.

There's another, wider archway, too, through which I glimpse a broad table covered with beakers, test tubes, sample cases, and implements of scientific study.

This lair, this home—it's chaos and beauty, order and abandon.

"*Ciel*," I breathe. "I love it. You live here?"

"I do. And sometimes the others join me. It is our shared haunt, where we do anything and everything we desire." The heat of his hand presses the small of my back. He leans close to my ear and murmurs, in a voice of dark, sugary sin, "Christine, what do you desire?"

My body buzzes with illicit delight, and my breath quickens. He slides his other hand across the exposed upper curves of my breasts, feeling their rise and fall.

I have never been touched like this.

A hot flush rolls over my body, and my nipples tighten. "Erik," I breathe.

"Who told you my name?" he murmurs.

"Matthieu did. You were not watching us last night?"

"I could not. If I had watched, I would have charged through that mirror, pulled him away, and fucked you soundly myself. But you were not ready. I needed him to prepare you, to help you get comfortable with a man's touch, with his tongue. You needed someone normal and beautiful, who would not frighten you."

"He is beautiful," I agree. "But so are you. And you do not frighten me."

"Don't I?" his voice at my ear sinks to a growl. "Maybe you should be frightened. I have brought you

133

down here, as a predator might seduce prey into his lair." He shifts behind me, his body molded to mine, his arms encircling me and his palms resting against my lower belly. "Yet you came with me, no protest, no plea for mercy. The lamb, willingly walking into the den of the demon. For I am no angel, as you have guessed by now."

"I cannot believe I was stupid enough to believe you might really be a spirit," I breathe. Warmth is swelling, surging through me, ignited by his hands as they shift across my stomach. "I was told the Opera House was haunted, you see. So I was all too ready to believe it. And I—I hoped my father might be looking down on me. That perhaps he sent someone to protect and guide me."

Erik sweeps his hand up my belly, stopping just beneath my breast. "I can be both protector and guide. I have opened your mind to music, to the madness of lustful delights. I have taught you to please yourself, both in body and talent, and I refrained from my own desire—I have not touched you until tonight. Even now I would withdraw if you asked. But you will not ask, because you want me inside you, Christine."

I am poised, paralyzed against him, every nerve sensitized and singing only for him. I am an instrument, vulnerable and still, my strings taut, vibrating at each gentle touch.

"You came with me tonight," he murmurs, "not because I enthralled or entangled you, but because you want to be opened. You want me to steal tiny mews of pleasure from your lips, to tantalize every inch of your skin until the eager sweat dampens your flawless body like dew."

His fingers find my neck, stroking, flushing my body with a fresh wave of heat. "You want me to elicit the purest notes of bliss from this beautiful throat. You want the instinctive melody of male and female, the primal rhythm of my cock pumping between your legs. Tonight, you and I will become one—you, the exquisitely crafted lock, and I the key."

He tugs my dress off one shoulder and grazes his lips along my skin. His mask scrapes me a little, and I shiver.

"I came with you because I want to know you," I say. "From the first sacrilegious poem you spoke to me, I wanted to understand you. You have unraveled the edges of what I know to be true. You've inflamed and allured me until I can think of nothing but pleasure. I am untaught in these matters, and perhaps too willing to let you guide me. Yes, I want this, but I fear it too."

The image of Raoul's honest, open face rises in my mind. Is he what I want? The polite courtship, perhaps ending in honorable marriage and comfortable wealth for the rest of my life? Or do I want the dark promises of this masked stranger and the two men who indulge in pleasure with him?

I disengage myself from Erik, moving away so I can think.

Once I yield to him fully, I cannot undo it. The bridge will burn behind me.

"There are things that I want," I tell him. "Music and pleasure, yes. But perhaps, later on, a life beyond. A comfortable life in the city, with a family. Walks in the park with our children on Sunday afternoons. Quiet evenings at home. A normal life." I swallow, summoning all my courage to continue speaking, as Erik's hands fall to his sides. "There is a man who can give me all those things. And you—what can you give me?"

This question is my power. I feel it changing the air between us.

Erik's golden eyes meet mine, and in them I read an aching desperation. His hands are empty, open, helplessness in the slope of his shoulders.

"I cannot give you those things," he says. "Not yet, and perhaps not ever. All I can offer is my mind, every facet of it, and my talents, of which I have many. I will devote them to you. I will sacrifice my own pleasure for yours. If it is a god you need—a muse, an Angel, a guardian, a hero—I will consecrate my entire being to that role. When you have nightmares, my voice will soothe them, and to your enemies, I will become the nightmare."

My breath catches in my lungs. My heart has never beat so fast in my life.

Erik takes a step toward me. "I can give you a family," he says. "Worshippers, men who are committed to your pleasure, to all your desires. Men who will defend you against any threat. And I can promise you a power you don't yet have the capacity to imagine, dreams of a brilliant future beyond the restrained existence of a Vicomte's wife."

Another step. His voice deepens with intensity, thrumming through my body. "Is that really what you want, Christine—a finely crafted cage like the one you left at Marchette? A life of curbing your natural passions, conforming to a society that will neither commend nor remember you? My darling, you deserve so much more."

Tears are pooling in my eyes—not because I'm losing some vague, expected notion of what I've been taught my life should be—but because I never thought words like those would be spoken to *me*, by anyone.

"I can be a little fool sometimes," I whisper. "Lewd and naïve by turns. Perhaps you'll be annoyed with me, and tire of me quickly."

"Never." He practically snarls the word with that lovely wicked mouth of his. "Once I take you, you're mine forever. Ours, if you like."

His. Theirs. Forever.

My whole body is trembling. I think I might shake apart from the storm of emotion, desire, and exhaustion. I try to blink away the fog clouding my eyes, but it only thickens, and my heart skitters into a more frantic pace. I'm losing my balance.

Erik catches me as I fall, cradles me against his broad chest. He carries me through the lair into a back room and lays me on a bed clothed in red silk. I'm dimly conscious of soft things being draped over me before I sink into oblivion.

13

ERIK

I could take her now, easily. Women do not need to be conscious during the ritual. In the past, some of my kind would drug the maiden so she would not feel any pain.

Not all of us fulfilled the ritual in such a barbaric way. Consent was important to most of the clans. And I want more than Christine's virginity—I want her loyalty, her strange blend of lewdness and innocence, her quick memory, her lithe body, her passion and eagerness. I love her affinity for role-play—it came to her so naturally from the moment of our first encounter, and I want to try out new roles with her. She is a natural submissive, but with just enough of the rebel in her spirit to make it interesting.

Beyond that, I want her talent—her incredible voice.

Yes, I want all of it, not merely some ritualistic bursting of her hymen to unlock my power. I would never rape an unconscious woman. I won't touch her, no matter how desperately I ache to access my birthright.

A darker side of me understands how easy it would be. Lay aside the blankets, lift her skirts. Push my cock inside her slit—she is probably still wet with arousal from earlier, when I touched her. I could break that delicate barrier inside her, fill her up with my cum. And that one simple act, sex with a human virgin, would unlock everything I'm capable of.

It is a powerful temptation. So I walk away.

I go to my organ, and I play. I play every song I've ever heard, and many that I've composed myself. Over and over I play them, faster and wilder.

Two hours after Christine falls asleep, Matthieu and Joseph appear in the shadows. They linger, watching me, casting significant looks at each other until finally I stop playing with a sigh and say, "What?"

"Did you?" Matthieu asks.

"Did I fuck her? No. She was too exhausted and overwhelmed."

"*Merde*," says Matthieu, tugging his lip ring with his canine. "I wanted to see your new powers."

"Erik, what did you do to the young Vicomte?" Joseph asks, his face sober.

"You mean after you allowed him access to Christine against my orders?" I shoot him a challenging glare, which he returns by lifting his chin defiantly.

"He left to get water for Christine," Joseph says, "and we didn't see him again."

"Oh, that. I thought you might defy me, and I wanted him distracted, so I poisoned one of his horses and sent a stable-boy to tell him about it. He cherishes his precious steeds, so of course he forgot all about Christine and fled to the stables."

"You poisoned a horse?" exclaims Matthieu. "Fuck, Erik. That's cruel."

"The mare will recover."

"Raoul will be back," says Joseph. "He seems a cheerful and honest fellow, but I sensed determination in him. He does not yield easily."

"My favorite kind of man." I look Joseph straight in the eyes, and his jaw clenches. His soft mouth curves up at one corner.

"Wait, wait." Matthieu leans on the organ, staring at me. "Erik, tell me you are not planning to seduce the Vicomte de Chagny?"

"Planning to? No." He sighs with relief, until I add, "I have already begun the seduction."

Matthieu knocks his forehead against the organ, his blond curls tumbling around his face. "Damn, damn, damn you, Erik. We don't need him."

"He has wealth, a title, and recognition among the nobility. He can help us. He's useful to me."

"And how do you know he'll succumb to your charms? Perhaps he prefers women."

"He likes men, too," interjects Joseph. "I had a moment to speak with him outside Christine's room."

"That's half the battle won, then. Remember how long I worked on you, Joseph?"

"I've heard this story far too often," moans Matthieu. "You two met when Joseph was sixteen, but of course being the upstanding bastion of moral fortitude that you are, you kept the friendship platonic until he turned eighteen, and then you began wearing him down over the course of six months."

"Whereas with you, it took only three days." I reach over and cup Matthieu's chin, lifting his golden head and leaning in to kiss his mouth. "Go to bed, both of you. I want to be alone when she wakes. I'll send for you when it is done. Joseph—stay a moment."

Matthieu pauses to kiss Joseph on his way out of the lair. When he's gone, I rise and approach my rebellious lover.

I'm taller than Joseph is, but only slightly. Still, I enjoy the physical dominance.

"Why?" I ask. "Why are you trying to sabotage this, Joseph? Warning her to stay away from me, letting her see Raoul? She nearly denied me outright tonight, on the scant hope that the Vicomte might marry her one day. You know what this event means to me, what her involvement could mean for all of us. This is my dearest hope, the one I told you about in secret when it was just the two of us. Remember? You and I, rutting in the dark, crying in each other's arms when it felt like the world was against us?"

"I remember," he says. "Erik, I did it for her. If she is going to choose this, choose *us*, she must do it with a full understanding of what it means. She must have options. You and I didn't have many options for comfort."

His words are an arrow through my heart's flesh, poison in my blood. "So you chose me because there was no one else. I was the piece of garbage that you made the best of, because you had no better option."

"No!" He grips my biceps in his large hands. "No, Erik! I yielded to you because I wanted to, because I admire you. I care about your wellbeing, your future. I love you. You know that. This works, with the three of us, because we love each other. It isn't only the games of pleasure I enjoy. I love you. I adore you, my Phantom, my wounded dragon."

His hand finds the edge of my mask, and he peels it away, baring my whole face. For a moment he takes me in, showing me that he accepts everything—every part of what I am.

Then he presses his mouth to my lips, and the hardened edges of my anger soften a little as I open to the kiss. His tongue slides in, swirls around mine in a slick curl that makes my cock tingle.

Joseph pulls back slightly, his dark eyes shining. "We have to love her like we love each other. And loving her means wanting the best for her. Giving her choices. Do you love her, Erik?"

"I—I want her for myself."

He strokes my cheek. "That's not love, and you know it."

"I care," I snarl. "I care about you, about Matthieu, about Christine. You might think me the worst of monsters, but I'll have you know that I gave her a choice tonight. I did not force her, either physically or emotionally."

He looks pleased with me, as a teacher might be pleased with a student who is improving—and I cannot allow that. I can't let him believe that I'm softening, that I am anything but the Lord of this place, the alpha to him and to Matthieu, the dragon of the hoard, the King of the Hill. The Phantom of the Opera.

"I did not force her," I repeat. "But I will if I have to."

"No." He shakes his head. "Erik—"

"Leave," I hiss. "And tomorrow, you and Matthieu must begin the next bit of work I've set for you—giving the foolish managers the idea for a masquerade ball. Do you understand?"

He stares at me, his handsome face tight with anger. "Careful, Phantom," he says, fitting my mask back into place. "Careful that you do not estrange the ones who love you best."

14

 CHRISTINE

When I wake, I can't remember where I am for a moment, and it's terrifying.

This happened to me at Marchette, not long after I arrived there. I would wake in a panic, barely remembering who I was, where I was—suffering with a horrible sense of dread and loss. Slowly the memory of my father's death would seep back in, and I'd recall how I was brought to live at the Marchette School.

I've learned that if I simply lie still and do not try to force the memories, they will come back on their own.

So I stay perfectly quiet.

Silken sheets under my palms. Soft blankets over me. Candles in the corner, illuminating the shapes of several life-sized statues—nude figures writhing in passionate embraces. An archway draped with sheer black cloth. And beyond that door, music rolling through endless echoing spaces—the most beautiful, wild music I've ever heard.

Mist, and music, and a man with a mask.

The Phantom. Erik.

Slowly I sit up. My head spins a little; I haven't eaten anything in many hours, and I need water, too.

Cautiously I rise. I'm still dressed. Still wearing everything I had on when I collapsed.

I shuffle to the door and sweep the coverings aside. In the center of the lair is the organ, from which the music is pouring in great, passionate waves. My entire body shudders with the swelling force of it, with the power of its beauty. This is music that makes me want to strip naked and dance.

I creep around the organ until I can see him— the unmasked half of his face. He bends low, then leans back, swaying to the song, caught up in his composition. I listen, enraptured, until the song trickles down to a glimmering handful of delicate notes which he plays over and over with one hand.

He looks up, giving me a distant smile. "You're hungry. Thirsty." He nods to a nearby tray, where sits a quarter of a cold roasted chicken, a shaker of salt, some grapes, and a wedge of cheese. There's a pitcher as well, filmed with condensation from the chill of the water within.

I pour some water and drink gratefully before diving into the food. I don't eat much, just enough to take the edge off my hunger. There is another kind of hunger tightening my skin, swelling my breasts, tracing ticklish fingers between my legs.

A pleasant life of wealth with Raoul could mean security and happiness. Or it could mean the same gnawing sense of loss I had when I woke up today—

because I cannot see a gentleman like Raoul allowing his wife to be a dancing girl or an opera star. That's simply not done by the wives of nobility. I would have to quit the opera, give up dancing and singing, just when I'm beginning to realize how much I love it and how much true potential I have.

I would have to give up sweet golden-haired Matthieu, with his talented tongue and his lovely laugh. I would have to abandon Joseph, whose perfect lips and sincere kindness have thoroughly charmed me.

And I would have to give up Erik himself—his exquisite voice, his skillful teaching, and the lecherous lessons I enjoy so much.

Perhaps the rest, food, and water have clarified my mind at last. Because I know what I want. When I think of the route that leads to Raoul, a creeping dread and uncertainty settles in my soul. The path leading to Erik and the others is uncertain as well, but it's an exciting uncertainty brimming with art, beauty, glory, and pleasure.

Erik said this place was designed to allow him and the others to act out all their desires. Maybe it's time I act out mine.

I abandon the food and move to stand beside the organ, leaning one elbow on it and watching the intensity of Erik's face as he plays. I inspect the edges of his mask—so closely fitted it must have been tailored precisely to his features. There is no sign of what he's hiding, except a strange texture along the lids of that eye, and a bit more of the same texture along his neck. But his cravat and collar hide that area too well—I can discern nothing clearly.

He pauses in his playing, laying his hands in his lap and meeting my gaze with calm resignation. "I will take you back to your room above."

"You watched me, didn't you? Every day. Through the mirrors in the chapel, in my bedroom, even in the dressing room. You were always there."

"I was." His lovely mouth hitches in a defiant sneer. "Does that enrage and frighten you?"

"It should," I say softly. "It was horribly inappropriate for you to spy on me. But from the beginning, the idea of you seeing me made me wet. I excused it, pushed aside the guilt I should have felt, told myself it wasn't sin if you were an angelic spirit floating invisibly in the room."

I walk up to him as he sits on the bench, until my skirts brush his knee. "But you had a body. Those groans I heard—they were you, feeling pleasure at the sight of me." I scrape my dress off one shoulder, then the other, tugging it down until the neckline barely conceals my nipples. "Did you touch your cock while I was displayed for you, Erik? Did the sight of me make you come?"

His jaw tightens, his gaze fixed on my breasts. "Yes. I came so hard, Christine. My cum stains the back of that chapel mirror, as does Matthieu's. He was with me on the night I first taught you about self-pleasure. I had to cover his mouth so you would not hear the sounds he made when he came."

Shifting my stance, I feel slickness between my thighs. "My pussy is wet, Angel," I murmur. "My panties are soaked."

"Stop." Erik shakes his head. "Joseph is right. I have to take you back. I have had time to think about it, and this is too soon, too rushed. You do not yet understand all the potential lives you could lead. Who am I to force you into one life, when you have other options before you? I would be no better than those who forced this dreary existence on me. Stop undressing, Christine—I have resolved not to bed you yet."

I'm unfastening my dress, peeling it down, sliding my arms out of the sleeves. I shimmy it down my hips and step out of it—unlace the corset's front, and lay it open, baring my breasts to his view. Then the corset is gone, too, and my panties fall to the floor. As I told him, they are soaked through.

I have never been fully naked in front of a man before. But the slow exposure I've been learning from the Angel of Music and from Matthieu has helped me overcome my natural shyness. Or perhaps I had very little natural shyness after all. Perhaps it was only my strict training at Marchette that made me reluctant to display myself.

Certainly I have no such reluctance now. I've never felt more free, more comfortable, more beautiful than I do as I stand before Erik, nude as the statues of the Opera House.

"Do you like my pussy, Angel?" I touch one finger to the seam between my legs.

"Your pussy is beautiful, Christine." His throat bobs as he swallows.

The power that Joseph spoke of—I feel it in this moment. I relish it.

I nudge my way between Erik's legs as he sits on the organ bench. My nipples are peaked, and my breasts hang heavy, every bit of their thin skin on fire, yearning for a caress.

"Touch me," I whisper. "Kiss me. Trust me with your body, and I'll trust you with mine."

Erik seizes my breasts in his hands, a firm, squishing caress that makes me sigh with ecstasy.

"You think to tempt me, little one?" he says in the clear, lovely voice of the Angel. "You are an untaught virgin. I know so much more of pleasure, desire, and restraint than you do." He lets go of a breast and drags his fingers between my legs, a rough upward motion that sends a spike of arousal through my abdomen.

He rises, gripping my nape and my waist, hauling my naked body against his clothed one.

"I see what you're doing," he says, low and vehement. "You're trying to get me to remove the mask. That's all you want, isn't it? To know my secrets. To indulge a schoolgirl's idle curiosity. What will you do, Christine? Gossip about me to your little dancing friends? I've had a few of them, you know. I've spoken to them, crept into their beds at their invitation, and fucked them in the dark dormitory while they writhed with silent delight."

"You're trying to make me angry and jealous," I gasp through my constricted throat. "Trying to scare me away. It won't work. I know you're offering me something you never gave them. I'm special to you."

"Being *special* can be a curse," he hisses. "I should know."

The hand at the back of my waist slides lower, cupping my bottom. His finger pushes between my ass cheeks, straight to the tight puckered flesh of my asshole. Another jerking pulse of arousal flies through my body.

Erik releases a smoky chuckle. "I will take every hole you have, little one. Are you ready for that?"

"Maybe not today," I whisper. "But yes. I want all the lessons from my Angel."

He leans in and crushes his mouth to mine, mask and all. He tastes like fire and smoke and spice. His kiss is music, seeping in my bones, unwinding all my muscles, liquefying every moral reason I ever had not to do this.

I whimper and press my bare mound desperately against the fabric of his pants, aching for friction.

"Needy little lamb," he growls. "Tell me what you want."

"I want you to fuck me," I breathe. "I want your cock to come inside my pussy."

Erik groans against my lips. "I will come so deep inside you." He lashes his tongue, hot and wicked, into my mouth. His arms close around me, a frantic, lust-mad grip, and with a single swift motion he scoops me up and carries me through the rear doorway into the bedroom, where he lays me on the bed before blowing out most of the candles.

In the hazy gloom he comes to me, his yellow eyes shining like pure honey, like captured sunlight. He takes off his tailcoat, unbuttons his vest, tosses aside his boots. But he does not remove his shirt or his pants.

"Your body is a poem," he says. "One day I will tie it with such beautiful knots, with braids and loops, all perfectly symmetrical. I will make you into a living work of art. I'll bind those breasts until they swell between the knots, and I'll leave your pussy open, so it can drip for me as you lie bound, immobile."

I have never burned so hot in all my life. I can feel the liquid sliding from my sex along my thigh, onto the bedding. I am a mess, and all for him.

Erik unbuttons his pants and pulls his cock and balls out through the opening. In the half-light I note how much larger his penis is than Matthieu's. It's thick and veined, with a broad head. A raw, strong, virile cock, hung with heavy balls, made for pumping cum into girls like me.

"You're the first virgin I've had," he says, running his ringed fingers along the generous length. "And the first with such exquisite talent. You're the first woman I've wanted to know and love for longer than a single night. I meant it when I said I will be the dread of your enemies, the protector of your dreams. I've waited for you, Christine, for longer than you know."

He crawls over me, and I whimper, lifting my hips. I've never done this, but I've imagined how it could work. I've dreamed of it. My body knows what to do, deeply, instinctively. He belongs inside me. I will make it happen.

But he kisses me first. His hot mouth meets mine, and I barely mind the hard edge of the mask. One of his canines is unusually sharp—I didn't notice that before. His tongue quivers between my teeth, searching out the roof of my mouth, flicking delicately against my tongue. His hand slides over my breast, cupping the heavy swell of my flesh, rubbing my nipple until I squeal softly, desperate.

Erik chuckles and smooths his hand along the flat of my belly, around the contour of my hip. He touches my sex, thumbing my clit gently, with a sigh of satisfaction. Then his hand sinks lower, and I turn my flaming face aside on the pillow, embarrassed at how soaked my pussy is.

But Erik groans with delight. "Christine, your body is a sinner's dream, a flood of desire. Arch your legs, sweetheart. I'm going to put my cock inside you, now. Just the tip, at first."

He rubs his cock head through the sloppy slickness, pats it against my swollen lips until I writhe with shocked arousal at the wet sound.

"Scoot back against the pillows," he orders. "And watch me enter you."

I obey, half-sitting against the pile of pillows, my body curved and my legs spread wide so I can look down and see the blunt head of his huge cock nosing into my pink flesh.

"Talk to me, Christine," he says. "You talk filthy so well, little one, despite your innocence, or perhaps because of it."

"Your cock feels so hot," I murmur. "Every time you touch my pussy with it, I feel these unbearable tickling sensations. Tingling, so much tingling— pleasure washing through my belly. My pussy feels swollen, flushed, sensitive—it wants to be filled with cock, with your thick, perfect cock, Erik. Please push your cock inside me."

With a shaking moan, he scoots even closer on the bed, lifting my legs and angling his tip, popping it inside my lips just a little before bobbing out again. The tantalizing motion is too much; I seethe in frustration, seizing his shoulders, trying to force him into me. My fingernails drag the blousy shirt off one shoulder, exposing his collarbone.

"Fuck me," I say, breathless. "Just fuck me, you devil."

He snarls, his teeth even whiter and sharper than they were before, his eyes so bright yellow they're practically glowing. He presses deeper, and I gasp, freezing around the girth of him.

"You're so big," I whisper. "Oh, Angel. It hurts a little, but I love it. More, please."

"More what?" he says hoarsely.

"More cock," I whine. "May I please have more cock?"

"Good girl. And you may, in a moment." He places one finger on my clit and swirls it in tiny circles, until I'm venting little sharp gasps in a frantic staccato. "Oh—oh—oh—" The orgasm crashes over me, surging and pulsing. He follows the rhythm, shifting deeper inside me between each convulsion of my pussy around his cock.

Some faint barrier of resistance in my body gives way—he thrusts gently until it yields and widens completely, letting his solid length fill me all the way up.

Immediately an intense vibration courses over my body, and I scream with the ecstasy of another orgasm flooding through my core, racing along every limb. Erik chokes, shoves even deeper into me. He groans, and his entire body shudders over and over. His cock pulses hot and violent in my soft channel—I can feel the spasm and twitch of his heavy balls against my bottom as he releases copious amounts of cum into my womb.

Something else is flowing into me, too—a quiet, thrumming energy I've never felt before, not even during my previous orgasms. It soaks into my bones, illuminates my nerves, brightens my mind. I feel strangely, beautifully awake—peaceful, perfect, satisfied.

"It's done," Erik gasps. "It's done, at last. I can't believe it. Fuck, Christine. Thank you."

Erik's cock keeps twitching, pulsing more cum, filling up my belly. I lie enraptured and nearly senseless on the bed, weakened from bliss.

He's still groaning and quaking with such abandon that the sound of him titillates my clit again. At last he pulls out of me, and I feel the warmth of his release dripping from my slit.

"Clench your pussy for me, sweetheart," he says, so I contract the muscles. "God, yes, I can see my cum oozing out of you, tinged with your virgin blood. Beautiful." He swirls his fingers in the mingled liquid of his cum, my blood, and my arousal, and he marks my belly with it—a strangely purposeful mark, like a sign. The lines of the mark burn warm for a moment before soaking into my skin.

"I've never spent myself so thoroughly in anyone," he murmurs. "I feel amazing. I feel—new."

He wipes himself on the blanket and puts his cock away, buttoning his pants again before reclining at my side and stroking my hair. "How do you feel, little one?"

"Refreshed," I murmur. "Wonderful. And—and I feel—claimed." I sneak a bashful glance at him.

"You *have* been claimed." His fingers glide along my belly, up between my breasts. "You've been marked by me."

"Sex can make children, can't it?" I ask. "Will I have your child?"

"No. I can't explain that yet, but rest assured, you won't get pregnant." He hesitates a moment. "Did you feel anything else? Anything that wasn't just pleasure?"

"I'm not sure." I frown a little.

"It doesn't matter," he says quickly. "There's plenty of time to discuss that." He drags a pillow under his head and sighs, letting his eyes drift shut. "God, I'm exhausted."

"Did you stay up all night while I slept?"

"I did."

"No wonder you're tired." I curve my naked body against his clothed one, feeling very naughty and delightful. "Should I put my clothes back on?"

"Mmm," is all he murmurs. Is he falling asleep? The savage beauty of his features seems to be relaxing into a drowsy softness.

He fucked me, and yet he refused to be naked with me. I desperately want to see more of him. I know with complete certainty that nothing he's hiding could change the tremulous tenderness I feel for him, the possessive ache in my heart, the desire to dismantle his walls and slip inside them.

If I take off the mask while he's sleeping, that barrier will be removed, and when he wakes with me still here, still smiling, he'll understand that I am devoted to this, no matter what.

The cadence of his breathing tells me he's sleeping now. The violence of his orgasm and his watchfulness have wearied him.

I ease myself into a sitting position. Gingerly I pinch the edge of the mask in my fingers.

And I pluck it away.

It resists a little, and there's a glimmer of strange light as it detaches, as if some mystical force held it securely in place.

What I see beneath it isn't scars or birthmarks, disease or decay.

I see flat scales, a dark, nearly iridescent green, like a deeply shadowed forest. Glossy scales lying so tightly against each other they're practically smooth, like a snake's skin. They begin at his hairline, covering half his face. The part of his nose that's usually concealed by the mask is flatter than a normal person's nose, with a slitted nostril. The scales circle his lips and continue down his neck, beneath the part of his shirt that I didn't pull aside. I can only imagine where else the scales might be on his body. Not on his cock, thankfully. And both his hands look normal.

His glossy black hair, usually so carefully arranged, has shifted, revealing his left ear—green, sweeping into a point.

The clues are solidifying, like bits of scenery finally assembled on a stage.

Scales and yellow eyes. Inexplicable mist, and the transformation of the mirror's surface into a portal. Supernatural occurrences, rumors of ghosts at the Opera.

Matthieu's smirking comment: *Mages got their power by forming an intimate connection to the dragons.*

The opera we've been performing tells of dragons stealing maidens and rutting with them. And it tells of mages sleeping with dragons to gain a share of their power.

Matthieu and Joseph are fucking Erik. And Erik just fucked me, a virgin.

Phrases he has spoken to me return to my mind, brimming with new meaning.

You are a virgin, yes? No man has touched you in that special place between your legs? Because only a pure-hearted virgin is worthy of my instruction.

I've waited for you, Christine, for longer than you know. You're the first virgin I've had.

It's done, at last. I can't believe it. Thank you.

Joseph warned me about Erik's plans—the danger of them. He was speaking of the danger of dragons, the danger of magic.

Erik is a dragon. Or part dragon, at least. I'm not sure how it works, but I vaguely remember hearing that dragons could shift into human form.

I thought dragons were extinct. I thought the mages had been cleansed from the world. Magic is wrong, twisted, dark, and wicked. It corrupts and consumes.

160

When the mages walked this earth, they did anything and everything for power and riches. They tortured and killed people for sport. The dragons captured and raped countless virgins, burned cities, and stole the contents of whole treasuries, leaving people to suffer and starve.

That is why the dragons and mages had to be destroyed, to create a pure and peaceful world.

Yet *this* dragon survived. He's been hiding here, beneath the Opera House, rutting with two men who are just as hungry for power as he is.

And I gave him exactly what he wanted.

With his mask still clutched in my hand, I fling myself off the bed and fall to my knees, retching.

The sound rouses Erik.

With a guttural cry of rage and pain, he springs from the bed, snatching a silken cord that hangs from one of the statues. A flick of his fingers, a twitch of his wrist, and the noose he just knotted flies over my head, tightening around my throat.

Erik steps behind me, hauling me away from the small spatter of vomit, jerking me upright with my back to his chest.

"Couldn't help yourself, eh, Christine?" he snarls. "Had to have a look under the mask. My condolences, darling. I can never let you go now that you've lied to me, broken my trust, and seen what I am."

I clutch the rope, trying to suck in a breath through its constricting circle.

"Why couldn't you have listened, Christine?" Erik's tone shifts to the angelic voice, a gentle spirit bemoaning my sins. "Now I will have to do terrible things to you."

15

CHRISTINE

The world is going dark. My whole head feels as if it's expanding, bursting—

The noose relaxes, and I haul in a life-saving breath. But I'm limp, pliable, helpless in the wake of the near blackout.

Erik snatches another coil of rope and begins to arrange my limbs, tying them into place quickly, deftly.

"I can't let you destroy all of this," he's saying. "Lives are at risk, Christine—mine, Joseph's, Matthieu's."

My arms are pinioned against my back, my breasts are cinched into bulging swells. My legs are bent, with ropes stretching from my knees to my shoulders, linked in such a way that my thighs must remain spread as I kneel.

"I won't tell anyone." I force the words out through trembling lips.

"But I can't trust you to keep your word. This is why I should have waited and not rushed into fucking you. I know so little of you, Christine. Are you the silly girl who would betray us, or the heroine we need, the anchor to which we may bind our wandering ships? Are you our doom or our safety?" He runs a loop of rope beneath my chin and fastens it so my head stays tilted slightly back. His fingers graze the column of my throat.

"You can trust me," I gasp. "I swear it."

I'm kneeling on the rugs, thighs apart, arms bound tight, my neck arched a little. Erik finishes his work and stands back to inspect it.

"Not my best," he says. "But it is pleasing."

Then he picks up the rug I soiled and carries it out.

He doesn't return for a long time, not until he has played at least three terrifying songs on the organ and a strident solo on a violin.

While I'm alone, trussed up in the elaborate net of rope, I have time to think.

The revelation was startling, yes. There is something monstrous about Erik's glossy scales, his yellow eyes, the left canine that's sharper and longer than the other. But as I ponder the situation, I realize that his monstrous aspect isn't what bothers me.

I'm more revolted by the secrets, the fact that he used me without telling me everything. Earlier, when I vomited, I was sickened, not by his face, but by the fact that I might be nothing more to him than a tool for power.

He should have told me what he was before he fucked me. God help me, I think I would care about him and crave him in any form—angelic, human, or dragon. Whatever metamorphosis he goes through, however many more things I discover about him, I will still want him.

And now that I've settled that in my mind, all I need is more information. When I encounter a new aspect of the world, I like to plunge in and learn everything about it—as I'm doing with music, performance, and sex. It's the same with dragons and magic and whatever else Erik is hiding.

Now that the door is open to me, I must know it all.

Erik strides back into the bedroom and lights all the candles with a simple gesture. The casual display of magic startles me, but I'm interested, too.

I can't help staring at his face. The contrast of pale, razor-sharp male beauty with sleek reptilian scales is fascinating.

"Horrific, isn't it?" He gestures to himself, teeth bared.

"Your appearance scares me less than your nature," I say. "Speak to me, Angel—help me understand you. You could have taken me anytime you liked, but you didn't. You seduced me. You let it be my choice. So that gives me hope you're not entirely evil."

"Not entirely evil?" He laughs, loud and wicked. "How kind of you, Christine. How generous. Yes, I'm well aware that humans believe every one of my kind to be irredeemably evil. We have a similarly sweeping opinion of humans—that they are all low, dull, untalented mud-creatures, grubbing about in their stolid, simple lives, terrified of anything that is bright, sharp, or different."

He sinks to his knees, facing me as I kneel in my bindings. "I thought you were special, with your purity and ignorance, your ache for sensual knowledge, your stunning talent, and your quick memory. But you react to me the same way they all do—with disgust and terror. Usually I kill the people who find out what I am." His finger traces the hollow of my throat.

"I am sorry for how I reacted," I tell him earnestly. "I was startled. I did not expect a dragon, of all things. I've been taught how terrible they are. But I was also taught that all men are vile and that sex is only for procreation—and none of that was true. Perhaps the teachings about magic and dragons were flawed also. Also, sweet Angel, not everyone is disgusted by you. Think of Joseph and Matthieu."

"They are unique among men." His voice softens.

"Are they mages?"

"Mages are simply humans with a capacity for magic. Think of it as a hook on which one may hang power. Not everyone is born with this hook, and so not everyone has the capacity for magic. Matthieu and Joseph both have the hook, and their intimacy with me allowed them to access a very minimal amount of magical power. An orgasm during sexual intercourse with a dragon enables the transfer of magic from one body to another."

He reaches out absently, fondling one of my breasts, which is squished outward, prominent and peaked because of the bindings. The slight pained discomfort of my position renders every bit of my skin wildly sensitive, and that casual touch on my breast ignites me. I feel as if Erik is guiding white flame lazily across my flesh, tracing it around my nipple. I whimper, feeling the tingle at my clit again.

"Did you give me magic?" I whisper.

"You had an orgasm with me inside you, so yes, you received a small dose of my power. If you possess the capacity for magic, that power will remain within you, and you'll be able to use it eventually, once you've accumulated enough of it during multiple trysts with me. If you have no affinity for magic, the energy will dissipate."

My stomach thrills and sickens. How wonderful it would be to have magic—and in a world like ours, where mages are killed, how very, very dangerous it would be.

I shift the line of my questioning. "Why do dragons need virgins?"

"When a young male dragon comes of age, he must rut with a human girl. The breaking of her hymen has a ritualistic, magical significance, and the act unlocks his inherited power. Until he fucks a virgin, the dragon has very limited access to magic."

"What about female dragons?"

"They are born with greater access to magic than males, though they can gain more power by mating with a fully unlocked male dragon." He reaches between my legs, running his fingers through the wetness gathering at my core. A devilish smirk crosses his face, mingled with a look of surprise and relief. "Still attracted to me, Christine? Or does being bound and naked make you wet?"

"Both." I squirm, panting. "What you said before, that you wouldn't get me pregnant—was that true?"

"You are safe from pregnancy. Dragons do not breed with humans." He dabs at my clit with the pad of his finger, sending a sprinkle of bright pleasure through my belly. "We go into heat now and then, but we only rut with our kind during that phase. My dragon father broke the law. He bred my human mother while he was in heat, and he was killed shortly thereafter, at the Battle of Berlin. I was born about nine months later, twenty-six years ago, not long after the Dragon Wars ended. My mother was wretchedly ashamed of me and kept me locked in a cellar for most of my childhood."

"That is horrible."

"Yes." He keeps nudging his finger between my pussy lips, delicately teasing me. "Fortunately she had inherited a sizeable library, so I had access to books."

My thighs are shaking. I want to press them together so badly. I need quick movement, firm friction, not the light brush of his fingertips.

But I do not beg. I try to control myself and listen.

"When my mother died, I nearly starved," Erik continues. "I'd never been taught how to apply my magic, but I manage to use a little of it to get out of the cellar. With beatings and long lectures, my mother had ingrained into my soul how ugly and despicable I was, how revolting and wrong, so I knew enough to hide my face as I wandered the human world. This place, beneath the Opera House, used to be a dragon's lair. I had a vague ancestral memory of it, passed on from my father, and I found my way here."

Meditatively he lifts his wet fingers and trails one across his gleaming tongue, tasting the liquid he has gathered from my pussy. "In this place I found volumes of dragon lore—not the distorted version humans tell, but our own records. And I found some treasure, enough to enable me to pursue certain cherished hobbies, like music, science, and invention. Enough for me to begin securing my hold on the Opera House."

Erik rises and walks to a framed object I had thought was another painting—but when he drags the covering off it, he's looking into a shining mirror.

He touches his scaly cheek, tilts his face, and traces the angle of his jaw. "I am stuck like this, unable to shift forward or backward—at least, not yet. Since I took your virginity, I feel changes in myself— but it will take time for my powers to fully develop. Eventually I hope to switch forms at will."

170

"And then what will you do?" I manage. "After your powers fully develop?"

"That, Christine, is something I will not tell you yet. I am still not sure that I can trust you."

"And I am not sure I can trust you either," I retort.

He turns around, his yellow eyes sparking. "So bold now, little lamb. Bleating your defiance at me while you drip your need on my carpet."

With a sudden graceful movement, he lies down on the floor, stretched to his full length, face-up between my parted knees. He scoots farther under me, but with my head tilted back, I can't see where exactly his mouth is.

"Erik," I whimper. "What are you doing?"

"You're a mess, little one," he says. "It's time to clean you up."

Erik's tongue slithers between my folds, probing and gliding. He laps thoroughly, slowly, cleansing every tender bit of flesh. When he begins to nibble my clit, I squeal with desperate need.

"Are you screaming because you need to come, or because a dragon is licking you?" says Erik calmly.

"Both," I breathe. "Erik, I don't think you're hideous. I think you're beautiful, even with the scales. Maybe because of them. Some part of me likes that about you."

"You're only saying those things because you want to come on my face." Another languid lick.

"And because you want me to release you from the ropes."

"I do want to come on your face," I whisper, half-ashamed of the words. "But I also think you're beautiful. I won't tell anyone, Erik. I care about you and the boys. I want so much more, from all of you."

"Tell me," he says, between savoring sweeps of his tongue. "Tell me what you want."

"I want you to fuck my pussy again." I tremble as bliss begins circling, circling through my lower belly, so near, yet just out of reach. "I want you to put your cock in my other holes, in my mouth and my ass."

"And what about Matthieu and Joseph?"

I close my eyes, losing myself to the lecherous dreams racing through my mind. "I want to kiss them, touch them, and make their cocks spray beautiful white cum. I want to watch you take them, in whatever way men take each other. And I want them to watch us. I want them to see you fucking me."

Erik's hot breath puffs across my sex. His voice is hungry and hoarse. "And do you want them to fuck your pussy, too?"

"Yes." I quiver, my pussy flexing desperately. "I want all of you to fuck me."

"And Raoul?" Erik kisses my clit, and I vent a breathless scream. "What if we all fucked him too?"

"He would never agree—"

"But if he did." He mouths my clit, humming deeply, and a blissful shock vibrates through me.

172

"Yes!" I cry, shaking. "Yes, I want that. I want everything."

"Good girl," says Erik, and he suckles my clit hard, still humming, letting the edge of his teeth graze the oversensitive bud.

I shriek, spirals of ecstasy shooting through my belly. Coming like this, when I'm bound tight and unable to move, is the most exquisite, defenseless kind of release. I keep screaming, and Erik keeps sucking and lapping and murmuring against my folds.

He moves out from beneath me, his lips and jaw gleaming wet.

But he isn't done with me.

He cups his hand over my sex, driving two central fingers deep into my pussy. And he begins pounding me with that hand. Squelching sounds fill the room as he hammers his hand into me, the heel of his palm smacking my sensitized clit. Wild bursts of pleasure explode through my belly, cresting until I come again, helpless, shrieking, my breasts swollen and needy, nipples painfully erect.

I never dreamed that anything could feel like this. It's as if my other orgasms were rehearsals, and the ones I've had with Erik are the main event. The opening night.

Opening night—

"God," I gasp, tears of bliss seeping from my eyes. "Erik, you must let me go. I have to star in *La Guerre* again tonight."

"I may have news about that," Erik says, thumbing the tears from my cheeks with his dry hand. "Shortly before you woke, Matthieu sent a note down the message chute. No, don't ask what the message chute is—I will show you later. According to the note, Carlotta was peeved by your wonderful success last night. She went to the managers and told them she would deign to return and sing the role for them, as a personal favor. And they agreed. So you are back with the chorus girls. Which means, yes, you have to perform, but you do not have to run off immediately. You have a little time to rest and recover. And you will not have the pressure of being the star tonight. But rest assured, after this performance I will make them reinstate you as leading lady."

"So you're going to let me go, after all?"

"Maybe." He strokes my hair back from my sweat-damp forehead. "Is that what you think I should do with you, little lamb?"

I look up at him, worshipful and utterly submitted. This is what Joseph meant, about finding his own power in yielding to Erik. There's a strange freedom in giving up my choices to the Angel.

"I came on your face," I whisper. "So it seems only fair you should come on mine."

Erik's golden eyes light up. "Again you surprise me, little one. You want your Angel to come all over this pretty face?" He pats my cheek, drags a finger along my lips. "What if I come on your sweet pink tongue?"

"Oh yes," I breathe. "Please come on my tongue, Angel."

My head is still tilted back, immobilized. Erik moves to stand beside me, angling himself until his crotch is level with my mouth. "Keep those pretty lips open."

His pants are distended with his erection. The moment he unbuttons them, his cock pops free, rigid and hot, poking its blunt head against my cheek. I feel the tiny wet smear of drops against my skin.

"You are wet, Angel," I murmur.

"That is precum, little one," he says. "Put out your tongue."

When I obey, he squeezes his cock head against the flat of my tongue, until I can taste the salty heat of the precum.

"Open wider," he says hoarsely, huffing as he begins to rub his length with quick jerks. "Look at me."

I angle my eyes toward him, watching his gorgeous features tense with passion, watching the flex of the glossy, scaly skin on the left side of his face.

Faster he strokes, groaning, his eyes gazing hungrily at my bound, naked body. I watch the tiny slit at the head of his cock as more beads of precum dribble out. I pant along with him, small mewling noises while he moans louder and louder.

He dips his cock partway into my mouth, angled so that its head thrusts against my cheek, pushing it outward. The heavy thickness of his shaft rests at the corner of my mouth.

Erik cries out, pushes my jaw wider, and sets the tip of his cock against my tongue. Hot liquid pumps over my tastebuds, flowing into the back of my throat. With another firm stroke of his fingers, he urges more cum out of himself onto my willing tongue. Open-mouthed, I work my throat, swallowing everything he gives me.

"Good girl," he gasps. "Such an obedient little lamb." He pats my face with the wet head of his cock, smearing cum along my cheek and temple. Then he kisses me. "I can taste myself in your mouth," he whispers. "Fuck."

A moment later he has tucked himself away again, and he's undoing my ropes. I slump to the floor, boneless.

After putting his mask back on, Erik picks me up and carries me into yet another room of this strange place, where there is an enormous sunken tub—more like a pool, probably large enough to fit a medium-sized dragon. At a wave of his hand, the water begins to steam invitingly.

He places my body in the sunken tub and rolls up his shirtsleeves, revealing more scales along his left forearm. He washes me methodically, carefully, from top to tail. When he's cleaning the lips of my sex, I begin to feel those warm swelling sensations again.

"Is it normal for me to want sex all the time?" I ask him.

"Male dragons have that effect on humans," he says. "Our pheromones are strong. It's an evolved tactic, designed to lure the female virgins we need, and to enhance our connection with the human males we fuck. You see, as much as we consider ourselves superior to most humans, we rely on them, too. Sexual intercourse with them helps to stabilize our control over our powers. It's a give-and-take, a symbiotic relationship. Most of us work for years to design our 'nest,' our carefully selected group of sexual partners. The ideal nest for a dragon consists of the first virgin he took and three or four male mages. Regular sexual activity keeps the nest strong and provides magical protections to everyone involved."

"So I'm part of your nest now?"

"Not just part of it," he says. "You are the core of it, the beating heart at its center, the sun around which the boys and I will revolve. I marked you with our fluids after we coupled, and the ritual will be complete once you've had us all."

The very thought of taking Erik, Matthieu, and Joseph heightens the warm tingle in my sex. "When will we do it?"

"Soon," he says. "I have a plan for it. I want the event to be special."

"So you're not angry with me anymore." I reach up and stroke the edge of his mask. He flinches a little, but he allows the touch.

"You've convinced me of your acceptance," he says. "At least for now. But I warn you, Christine—don't cross me, or betray me. I am merciless to my enemies."

16

My last visit to the opera did not end well. I meant to spend more time with Christine, but then one of my mares became ill and I had to leave abruptly.

I have hopes that this night will end better. The managers have informed me that Christine is no longer the lead, thanks to a new arrangement they made with La Carlotta. That displeases me, but at least Christine will perhaps be less overwhelmed and tired tonight. Perhaps she will agree to go to a late supper with me after the show.

I watch the first act from Box 2, cringing at the pompous vehemence with which Carlotta delivers the lines. Her voice and range are good, but her vibrato is too heavy, her mannerisms too fake. Her vanity and conceit is practically tangible.

Messieurs Richard and Moncharmin are sharing Box 2 with me again, as if they think they need to constantly entertain the patron of their theater. They quickly become inebriated and silly, and between them and La Carlotta, I cannot wait for this performance to be over.

The dancing chorus girls leave the stage, along with Christine. They won't be back for a while, and I have no reason to pay attention until they return, so I rise and leave Box 2, intending to stretch my legs.

I wander the velvety, candle-lit halls and staircases, inhaling the scent of roses and lilies from the overstuffed urns along the corridor. There's a familiar scent of sweetish smoke, too, like the weed I enjoy with my friends at the track sometimes.

Intrigued, I follow the fragrance, pausing when I find it most pungent outside the door to Box 5.

Could it be that my mysterious companion from the previous night is in here?

I lift my hand, preparing to knock, but then I pull it back. What would I say to him? Should I ask him if he's a ghost? Apologize again for drinking his liquor? Request a pull at the pipe he's smoking?

"Don't be an idiot, Raoul," I hiss under my breath.

As I'm turning away, the door to Box 5 opens and a hand catches me by the collar, pulling me inside.

The door closes. Once again it's thickly dark in the back of Box 5, but thanks to the light filtering in from the stage, my eyes adjust quickly.

A cloaked figure stands beside me, his gloved hand lifted, holding a pipe that trails smoke.

"Is—is smoking allowed in here?" I squeak. And then I despise myself deeply for sounding like a schoolboy.

The cloaked man rumbles a laugh. "You're adorable, Vicomte. I see you've managed to keep your pants clean today." His other hand lands between my legs, squeezing lightly before moving away.

I suck in a sharp breath. "Hands off, sir."

"As you wish. Have a seat, and I'll light a pipe for you. It's the best weed to be had in this entire region. I don't partake often, since I like to keep my faculties sharp—but this is a special occasion."

I hesitate. I should go back to Box 2, with the pesky inebriated managers. Or I could remain here and smoke with this strange companion. The weed will no doubt make Carlotta's strident vocals more bearable.

"Very well." I take the seat he indicates, and he seats himself next to me, so close our sleeves brush with every movement.

After packing and lighting a second pipe, he hands it to me. I suck gratefully, holding the fragrant warm smoke in my lungs a moment. When I release it, my companion pushes back his hood, leans over, and sucks my exhaled smoke into his own mouth.

In the half-light, I can see his face. The side furthest from me is half-covered with a white mask. The near side is strikingly handsome—he is sharp-jawed, with high cheekbones and long, inky lashes

182

beneath a neatly arched brow. His eyes are an odd color—yellow, almost luminescent, like a cat's.

Strange as his appearance is, it's a relief as well. This is a *man*, not a ghost. A man of flesh and blood—rather good flesh, probably, judging by what I can see of his body's shape.

My brain is beginning to swirl pleasantly, warmth tingling through my limbs. A delightful weed, as he said. Most effective.

The door of the box opens, and I startle, fearing that perhaps the managers have come to find me. But the figure that emerges is a young man, lean, muscular, and bare-chested, with a painted face and gold caps on his nipples. A gold ring graces his lower lip.

My cock twinges at the sight of him.

"This is Matthieu, a dancer in the opera. He plays the role of a slave-boy belonging to the dragon," says my companion. "He does not have to be onstage again for thirty minutes, so he has come to visit me. I hope you don't mind if I partake of a little indulgence while I smoke. Carlotta's performances are so tedious."

"Of course," I say. "I'm the one intruding—this is your box, and you may do as you like."

"Not an intrusion at all," says the masked man. "You're my guest."

I wait for the young man to produce some kind of drug, perhaps another fine bottle of whiskey—but instead, he steps past me, wafting vanilla scent into my nostrils. My masked friend moves his legs apart, and the young dancer kneels between them.

Before I can fully realize what is happening, the dancer unfastens my companion's pants and releases his cock—a thick, heavy member, half-erect. The dancer vocalizes a hum of pleasure and begins eagerly mouthing the bulbous head of the cock.

"Ah," sighs my companion, leaning back. "This is the way to watch the opera, eh Vicomte?"

I cannot speak. Frantically I take another pull at the pipe, while my own cock lifts involuntarily at the sight of the dancer Matthieu taking more of my companion's length into his mouth.

The shadows of Box 5 conceal what is happening from anyone else, but I can see it well enough. Matthieu runs the cock deep into his throat, then pulls off again with a wet slurp.

"Quiet, my love," says the masked gentleman, stroking the dancer's blond curls.

"Would you like me to pleasure you next, Vicomte?" asks Matthieu, looking up at me with wet lips and sparkling green eyes.

"*Mon Dieu*," I whisper. I can't reply with any other coherent words. I can barely move. I should leave.

Yet I stay. I watch the dancer shrug and go back to enthusiastically sucking on cock, while the masked man begins to stiffen and moan.

My penis is standing straight up now, tenting my pants. Too late to leave now—I cannot exit Box 5 in this condition.

"Ah, there is our Christine coming onstage again," says my strange companion. "She is such a beautiful dancer. The way her body moves—so sinuous, so flexible. One could almost imagine her being fucked as she dances. See there—as her leg lifts—ah. Perfect access."

He glances over at me. Reaches out to touch the prominent tip of my cock, which is prodding my pants. "You should take care of that, Vicomte. You can't be walking about the Opera House with an erection like that. Allow yourself some relief. Don't be shy—ah, gods, Matthieu, your mouth is magic."

Matthieu chuckles, and the throaty vibration makes my companion tense. "Fuck, I'm coming, Matthieu. I'm coming."

I try not to watch. But a sidelong glance shows Matthieu swallowing while the thick cock pulses and throbs between his lips.

With a low cry I tear open my trousers, pulling out my own dick.

"That's it," breathes my companion, still panting from his climax. After a moment, he keeps speaking to me in a low, warm, confidential tone. His voice is like honeyed smoke. "Think of Christine, Vicomte. Imagine that you're walking onto the stage right now, before all these people. You seize her in your arms. She is shocked to see you, but you can see the heat in her eyes. She is half-naked already, in that seductive little costume. You tear aside the bits of clothing, revealing her nubile body to the audience. They gasp, because she is so ripe, so beautiful. You lay her down on the stage and hold her thighs apart so they can all see her sex."

The dancer Matthieu crawls between my legs, runs both hands up my thighs. His fingers are laden with rings. The gold paint on his mouth has smeared, and his tongue flicks over the lip ring suggestively. "Yes, Raoul?" he whispers.

One word escapes me. The wickedest one I've ever spoken. "Yes."

His mouth envelops my cock. Warm, wet suction. I release a shaking breath, gripping the armrests of my chair.

My companion's strong hand clasps over mine, a supportive gesture, linking us in this fantasy. I can see what he's describing—Christine lying pliant and naked on the stage, her legs open to all.

"Her pussy is slippery with want," whispers my companion. "Her breasts are soft and warm. You touch them, press them, suckle them. Then she turns over, propped on hands and knees, her ass and her wet slit aimed toward the crowd. Your cock slides into her easily."

Matthieu's cheeks suck inward as his head bobs, pumping along my length, his lip ring and his tongue sending sparks of hot pleasure along my nerves.

I lift my gaze and see Christine with the other chorus girls, her body undulating and twisting. She is dancing with unusual abandon, with a seductive flair I hadn't thought her capable of.

"You thrust into Christine's sloppy wet slit again and again," says my companion. "Deeper inside her, until you fill her up—"

"With my cum," I whisper, and my hips jerk upward, my balls tightening as I release into Matthieu's mouth. He hums around my shaft, drinking me down. I cry out and the sound is muffled instantly by the masked stranger's palm.

"Hush, Vicomte," he murmurs at my ear. "We wouldn't want to disturb the other guests."

I cannot believe what I'm doing. I'm coming in a stranger's mouth, while another stranger muffles my cries of release. I can barely hold onto the pipe in my hand.

Matthieu licks my cock clean and puts me neatly back into my pants while I gasp and tremble with mingled pleasure and horror.

"A delight, Monsieur," he says, with a final pat to my crotch. Then he kisses the masked stranger on the mouth before leaving Box 5.

"What have I done?" I whisper.

"You enjoyed a little pleasure," says my companion. "As you deserve. Now hush, Raoul, and smoke your pipe." He pats my knee.

Dazed, I obey him. Soon, the sweet spiciness of the pipe forms a blessed haze in my mind, softening my guilt.

On the small table where the drinks were set the other night, there's a tray with a pipe holder. I set my pipe into it and lean back. Strange how Carlotta's voice seems more mellow now, almost like a lullaby. I will pretend this never happened. I never met with any masked stranger, never smoked a pipe, never had my dick sucked while a man breathed wicked fantasies about my sweet childhood friend.

None of this happened.

My eyes blink open.

The last act is nearly over, and there is no tray, no pipe, no masked stranger. Nothing but me, alone, in an empty box that smells only of roses.

Did I dream it all?

When I return to Box 2 and to my managers, I feel dizzy and confused. The only lingering proof of anything that occurred is the warm, sated feeling of my belly and balls. I have been thoroughly pleasured this night.

The managers are drinking coffee, and they seem much less drunk and far more disturbed. At first I think perhaps they heard some rumor of what happened in Box 5, but then they wave an envelope in my face.

"Do you know what this is?" Moncharmin shouts. "The damned 'Opera Ghost' again. He is incensed because we have not paid his so-called salary, and because we demoted Christine Daaé and returned Carlotta to the leading role! He says that if we do not put Christine back in the lead and pay him what we owe, he will cause some terrible catastrophe!"

"He's a prankster, a blackmailer," interjects Richard. "Apparently the former manager used to pay him off regularly, just to prevent any mischief around here. Well, we won't be bilked and cheated by some roguish beggar."

"I'd thought perhaps it was you, Vicomte," says Moncharmin. "Since we heard Christine was a friend of yours—I thought perhaps you were trying to push her career to new heights."

"But then I reminded him that you have no need to ask for money, like this fellow does," Richard cuts in.

"It wasn't me," I reply. "Though this turn of events is disturbing."

There is some connection between Christine and the Phantom of Box 5. I can feel it. I only hope it has not gone any further than his obvious admiration of her.

"I will speak with Miss Daaé tonight and find out if she knows of anyone who could be perpetrating this fraud," I tell them. "In the meantime, do nothing. I do not approve of the money I donate going into the pockets of some thieving wretch. It should all go to the arts, and especially to the young dancers with little means of support."

I swallow hard, thinking of Matthieu's mouth on my cock. He seemed to enjoy the act so thoroughly— savored me, swallowed me as if I was a choice wine. God, I am getting hard again. Why is this happening?

A roar of applause startles me. The performance is over, and everyone is cheering La Carlotta. Whenever the applause begins to die down, she lingers expectantly, curtsying until they begin clapping again. After two encores, the tenor Piangi leads her offstage with an apologetic smile.

I didn't order a bouquet this time. I have nothing to offer Christine. But I need to see her. Perhaps her presence can ground me, convince me that I'm not losing my mind.

She's not in the diva's suite tonight, so I must wait outside the shared dressing room where all the female cast members change. Women and girls emerge, simpering, giggling, cooing my name when they see me. I wave and smile at all of them, until at last no more women appear. Christine must be the last one left. Unless I missed her?

Cautiously I push open the door, rapping gently as I lean inside. "Christine?"

She's near the end of the room, standing before a full-length mirror. When she turns to face me, blood rushes to my cheeks—and to my cock.

She's wearing a pair of lace pantalettes. Her breasts are bare.

"Raoul," she says. "I thought you might come to see me."

For a moment I stand paralyzed, consuming her lush curves with my gaze. And then I remember that I am supposed to be a gentleman. Honorable, pure of heart, intent on making a difference in this city.

"What in God's name are you doing?" I snatch a robe from a nearby chair and hurry to wrap it around her. "Anyone could have walked in."

"And?" She shrugs, smiling up at me. There's something different about her tonight—a wild exuberance, an unfettered grace.

I hold her close for a moment, with my arm wrapped so tightly around her back I can feel her heart beating rapidly. So much for finding safety in her, settling my soul with her familiar presence. Her scent is different—spicier, deeper, velvety like the red depths between the petals of a rose. Her breasts are full and heavy against my other arm, the nipples tight and eager. A soft flush tinges the delicate skin of her chest. She's aroused. If I wanted to act out my fantasies upon her body, she might allow it.

I planned a slow, proper courtship with her. I've thought about it all day, decided how I would proceed—visits and dinners, luncheons and promenades. I would enchant her with my world of wealth, draw her away from the seductive glory of the Opera House. And then, when she was comfortable with me again, I would ask for her hand.

All my plans now lie jumbled in my head. I'm left with an odd pang of loss, an unsettled feeling, and a roaring desire in my soul, the violence of which surprises me.

A week ago I turned up my nose at Charles for fucking a barmaid in a back hall. Now I feel as if I'm a moment away from fucking Christine on her dressing table.

"You used to care about purity and propriety," I murmur, half to Christine, half to myself. "What happened to you?"

"I met someone," she whispers. "The Angel of Music. Or as some call him, the Phantom of the Opera."

Shock, realization, and rage blaze through me. If the depraved entity I met in Box 5 is the Phantom of the Opera—if he has been influencing my sweet Christine the way he corrupted me—

"What has he done to you?" I grip her upper arms. "Christine, darling, there is no angel or phantom. Just a very disturbed man with lecherous leanings and no sense of decency."

"You've met him, then," she says triumphantly. "He hinted as much."

"Christine," I say through clenched teeth. "If he has hurt you—"

"He hasn't forced me into anything." But her cheeks flush a telltale pink.

"Where is he?" I exclaim. "I have a message for the bastard."

"I have no doubt he will be here soon, if he is not already listening."

"Very well." I raise my voice a little. "Tell him I will have satisfaction for your honor. The back courtyard of the Opera House, behind the stables. One hour."

I rush out of the room, heedless of Christine calling my name.

This fiend is masquerading as a phantom to defraud my theater. He tricked me into debasing myself with a stranger, lured my sweet, innocent Christine into his web of debauchery. I will address the matter as I've been taught to do, as is the custom for men of my rank. A duel. I will kill the monster, or at the very least wound him so deeply he'll think twice before trying to seduce upstanding citizens like myself or vulnerable girls like Christine.

She has no one to protect her. I alone stand between her and utter ruin.

I'm an excellent swordsman—I have no doubt I will be the victor. And after the duel is done, I will propose to Christine. I will marry her, to save her honor and mine. Once we are married, we can take satisfaction in each other and put aside all this confusing nonsense about phantoms with masks and handsome dancers with hot, wet mouths.

It's autumn, and a cold wind spirals through the back courtyard of the Opera Lajeunesse. A few lanterns are still lit, enough to see by, but everyone has either gone home or retired to rooms and common areas within the main building. The Phantom and I will have this area to ourselves for the duel.

I borrowed a sword from one of the security guards at the Opera House. Since I'm the patron and a noble, the man didn't ask questions. The sword is a good one, a little different from the one I favor at home, but it should do the trick of slitting and skewering a licentious Phantom.

If he shows up at all.

I'm wearing a cloak over my tailcoat, and it billows around me as I wait. Leaves skitter across the cobbles, settling near the walls of the stable. Out here, the charred scent of woodsmoke mingles with the heavy animal smell from the stables. But each blast of chill wind freshens my face. I feel more alive than I've felt in months. Ready for action, for passion, for conflict.

"Monsieur le Vicomte."

My body responds to his voice, a heated chill surging up my spine, through my cock. Damn him.

I turn around. He's striding across the courtyard, with Christine at his side. She's clad in a voluminous red cape. Her brown curls spill from the hood over her breasts.

"Raoul, don't do this," she says, in that sweet, familiar voice I've loved since childhood, and again my body thrills. How can I be so attracted to both of them? It goes against everything I've been taught. A respectable marriage to a woman of good birth and good reputation—that is what I am supposed to want. Not the masked man in the great black cloak, with his sharp, slanted features and burning eyes. Not the woman who has so obviously slept with him, who appears now in his company, acting as if I am the aggressor rather than her savior.

"Are you on his side, then, Christine?" I hate that I sound a little lost, a little uncertain.

"No, sweet Raoul." She hurries up to me, laying her delicate hand against my cheek. "I am not on either side. And I'm always your friend. More than a friend, if you'll let me."

I turn my face inward, toward the skin of her inner wrist. She smells like lilacs, like honeysuckle. "He has soiled your honor, Christine."

"I'm not soiled." A quiet defiance stirs in her eyes, so different from the gentle girl I knew. Part of me likes the new Christine better. Her self-assurance is powerfully attractive to me. I wish I had half her confidence.

But I steel myself with the laws of society, as they've been imparted to me. "Ready yourself, Phantom," I demand. "Christine, stand to one side, please. This will not take long."

"Won't it, though?" The Phantom draws a rapier, inspecting its blade. "I've watched great masters teach swordplay to actors at the Opera, and I've practiced with two friends of mine. What's more, I've had to fight for my own life at three different times, with this very sword, and each time I killed my opponent."

"Raoul." Christine's voice is shriller now. "Stop this. You're being a fool. I understand that you're distressed—he told me how he has behaved toward you, and I think he could have handled things differently. But that doesn't mean—"

"You *told* her?" My voice cracks.

He told her how I came in that dancer's mouth.

I can't bear that anyone else knows, most of all Christine.

"It's all right," she says softly. "The way you've been raised—it isn't the only way to find happiness, Raoul. There can be joy, and freedom—"

But I'm barely listening. Blood thunders in my ears, and with a cry of shamed rage I leap for the Phantom, striking at him with all my force.

He parries my blow easily, knocks it aside as if it were nothing. But I'm on him again, faster than he must have expected. He jumps back, and we go at it in a frenzy of blows. The clash and ring of our blades echoes through the courtyard.

I drive him back, all the way to the overhanging porch under which the horses' hay is kept dry. He circles one of the posts, grinning at me beneath his half-mask. The lantern light flashes on his glossy black hair. I want to rumple that neatly arranged hair.

"Why?" I choke out, pacing to the right as he circles left. "Why did you do this to me? To her?"

"You act as if I've committed some great crime against both of you," he says. "I've done nothing but awaken each of you to your true desires. Those longings were dormant until now, but they were always inside you." His tone shifts into a gentle cadence. "There is nothing to be ashamed of, Raoul. You and Christine and I—we are attracted to each other, compelled not only by natural lust but by emotional affinity. You are not only someone we want, Vicomte—you are someone we need."

"I am not attracted to you," I gasp. "You monster."

The Phantom glances down at my trousers, which are prominently stretched around my erection. "Your body says otherwise."

"I am sometimes aroused by fighting," I retort. "And there is a beautiful woman present, who recently showed me her breasts."

"They are fine, are they not?" he says, with a companionable grin. "One for each of us."

From her vantage point near the hedge, Christine makes a small sound. I glance at her, and she bites her lip, her cheeks rosy, her fingers slipping under her cape to massage her breast.

"Look what you've done to her," I say. "You've turned her into a whore."

The Phantom's smile vanishes. He charges me, and I barely manage to block his attack. Then, with a deft sidestep, he swings his body and grips my wrist painfully tight.

"Apologize," he growls.

His thigh is between mine. My cock swells and hardens further, especially when I look at Christine and she's watching with hunger in her large eyes. She looks so beautifully innocent, yet wickedly wanton at the same time.

Perhaps, after all, he only did what she wanted. Does that make her a whore? If it does, then I am no better.

"I am sorry, Christine," I say.

The Phantom shoves me away, and I recoil, panting. This time I attack more carefully, and I succeed in driving him back against the stable. Or perhaps he lets me do it. He seems to be moving more slowly now, less intent on defeating me.

His back hits the stable wall, and I move in, grinding my sword against his blade. My hips are aligned with his, and as I press inward, my erect cock nudges against an equally hard shaft beneath his pants.

I freeze, my muscles straining as both of us struggle to keep the other's sword at bay.

The flex of his body, the male power radiating from him—it's like nothing I've ever felt.

His hips tilt, and he rubs his erection against mine. "Raoul." His voice is a low purr. "Draw your sword."

I glance at my weapon, still locked against his.

"Not that sword," he murmurs. Slowly he eases the pressure against the blade, and I do the same. I am lost again, dazed, falling down into the lovely wicked darkness.

The sword slips from my hand. Clatters on the cobbles.

His pelvis and mine, pressed together.

He reaches between us and carefully unfastens my pants. Pulls my cock out. The cold air strikes my burning skin like the bite of a serpent.

He's taking out his own huge cock, so much bigger and meatier than mine. With a gloved hand he presses them together, my heated skin flush with his. I can feel every inch of him against me.

"Christine, love," he says. "Come here."

She approaches, her face scarlet and her eyes alight with lust.

"Lick off Raoul's precum, would you, sweetheart? And mine as well."

She bends, holding back her brown curls, and bathes our cock heads with her pink tongue. I groan, trembling.

"I don't know why I keep doing this," I whisper. "Why, Christine? What is wrong with me?"

"Nothing, you sweet man, nothing." She rises on tiptoe and kisses my mouth, while the Phantom begins to rub both our cocks slowly. Thrills skate along my length, swirling in my stomach while Christine keeps kissing me, welcoming my tongue into the heat of her mouth. Her tongue slides between my teeth as well, softly questing, lapping, cherishing me.

"Raoul," she whispers against my lips. "You are one of us. You were always meant to be mine, and I am his, and he's also mine. Let us love you."

"But who is he?" I gasp through the growing pulses of pleasure.

The Phantom clasps the back of my neck with his other hand, and Christine shifts aside, smiling, so he can kiss me. He tastes of spice and smoke and darkness, the most delicious kind of beautiful hell.

"I'm the Angel of Music to Christine," he says. "The Angel of Power and Safety to others. To you, I am the Angel of Purpose. And I can give you the two things you lack in life—a family bound by sex and love, and a goal worth pursuing."

His hand tightens around our cocks. He leans his forehead against mine, huffing harsh breaths.

I can feel everything I've planned crumbling—the well-structured life I laid out for myself flattened, crushed, blown away like autumn leaves on the wind. The destruction of that future doesn't pain me nearly as much as I thought it would.

Suddenly, I feel as if I can breathe, and I do breathe—deep lungfuls of the crisp autumn night, laced with the dark licorice-and-roses exhale of the Phantom. I kiss him, tentatively, then harder.

Christine is behind me now, holding her body against mine, one hand cupping my bottom. The sensation of her small hand on my ass is driving me insane.

"Do you want her, Raoul?" pants the Phantom.

"Yes, god," I groan.

"Yes, *Angel*," he corrects, rubbing faster.

I can barely think through the hardness of his bare cock against mine. "Yes, Angel."

"And Raoul—" my name is a primal snarl from his lust-hoarse throat— "do you want *me*?"

"Yes—yes, Angel!"

"Fuck, yes," says Christine's sweet voice, and I come hard, my dick flinching and spurting uncontrollably.

The Phantom tenses and groans. White cum overflows from his cock, pouring along my shaft, slicking his black glove. He keeps stroking both of us with the slickness, until I'm so sensitive I can't bear it.

Then he backs away, stripping off his soiled gloves. His glorious cock hangs spent from the opening of his black pants.

"That was so beautiful," Christine murmurs, hugging me from behind. "I'm so wet, Raoul."

My cock twitches faintly at her words, but it's going limp. It will be a little while before I recover.

Twice today, I have come in front of two other people. And this time, strangely, I don't feel the same guilt. I feel purged, sated, awakened.

Christine comes around to my front and takes my softening cock in her hand. "It's beautiful, Raoul," she says. "Well-groomed and elegant, like you. I will be glad to take it in my pussy soon."

"God, Christine." My shoulders slump as she puts me away and closes my trousers. Then she wraps an arm around my waist.

"Come with us," she says. "There is somewhere we want to take you. You can rest, eat, and drink. Later, if you like, we can play again."

17

CHRISTINE

In the Phantom's lair deep beneath the Opera House, Erik and Raoul talk long into the night, while I drowse nearby on a sofa. Once I awaken a little, blinking at the two of them. They're kissing again, and Erik's hand is moving inside Raoul's pants. I smile, letting my eyes close.

The next time I awake, it's because of anxious voices.

I sit up foggily, rubbing my eyes. On the couch opposite me lies a horribly bruised man with blood in his golden hair. Joseph is arranging his limbs carefully, tucking a pillow under his head.

"Oh god," I gasp. "Matthieu!"

I fly to his side, and I almost take his hand—but it's swollen and bruised, as if someone stamped on it. His beautiful face is unrecognizable—puffy and mangled, with blood lacing his cheekbones, jaw, and forehead. More bruises bloom darkly along his bare chest and side.

"Who did this to him?" I say sharply.

"One of the Opera House guests was knocked unconscious and raped in an alley the other night," says Joseph. "The man who was escorting her home swears he was also knocked out, by a man matching Matthieu's description. But it couldn't have been Matthieu. He was with me that night—all night, since immediately after dinner. And he wouldn't do such a thing."

Joseph lifts shaking fingers to pinch the bridge of his nose, squeezing his eyes shut. A tear slides from beneath his lashes. "I'll wager the man who escorted her did the evil deed himself. But the woman's brothers believed his story. There's no proof for the magistrate to act upon, so the brothers decided to beat up the man they thought responsible. Matthieu was nearly dead when I found him."

"He needs a hospital," says Raoul shakily. He's standing to one side, his pants still undone. Beneath his mop of auburn waves, his pretty face is white as salt. I feel for him—he has been through a lot this evening—but right now, Matthieu is the priority.

"Erik may be able to heal him," Joseph says. "Since Christine unlocked his magic."

"Unlocked—his what?" quavers Raoul.

"Fuck," Joseph says. "Christine, I know Erik told you everything—I assumed he explained everything to the Vicomte as well."

I wince. "Not that I've heard. Though I've been asleep."

"What is happening?" Raoul says plaintively.

205

Joseph swears again. "Since I found you down here all together, I assumed he knew. Well, it's out now. See here, Raoul—I don't have the time or patience to tell you what we're talking about." He fumbles around on a bookshelf and selects two dusty, leatherbound volumes. "Here. Read these. About the dragons, and the Dragon Wars, and the mages. They will explain everything. Mostly."

"Everything, mostly," echoes Raoul. "Well, all right."

He plops onto a sofa and opens the first tome.

"Where is Erik?" I ask Joseph.

"Getting supplies."

I lean over Matthieu, carefully shifting aside a lock of his hair. "Poor darling."

"It makes me angry," Joseph says in a choked voice. "Matthieu is the sweetest, softest, most joyful man I know. I want to kill the people who did this to him."

"Don't," I tell him, horrified.

"Oh, I won't. Erik will."

At first I think he's joking, until Erik stalks back into the room, carrying a rack of vials, all different colors, and some kind of geode on a string. The unmasked side of his face is taut and flushed, and every line of his body is hard with rage. He looks, in a word, murderous.

My stomach drops.

We all back away, giving Erik plenty of space as he leans over Matthieu. He works in silence for a long time, and from my vantage point I'm not quite sure what he's doing. But Raoul, who is craning his neck from his seat, says, "Good God," in a very dramatic tone, so something must be happening.

At last Erik rises, sweeps his cloak around him, and strides away without a word, along the edge of the canal, into the darkness.

Joseph and I both leap to Matthieu's side.

The bruising on his chest, stomach, and ribs has receded, and the little that remains is much lighter. The cuts on his face look far better, as if they've been healing for days already. The swelling of his eye, lips, and jaw is also much improved.

Raoul is babbling semi-coherently. "It's not possible, magic is against the law. Can't have magic without dragons, can't have dragons without mages, I don't understand—where are the dragons? The dragons are dead. Healing magic doesn't exist. No. It's too much—I can't. I just can't."

"Shall I knock him on the head?" asks Joseph pleasantly.

"He's had to adjust his whole world tonight," I say. "Give him a little time."

"You've adjusted well, and quickly too." Joseph sheds a warm smile over me, and my heart flutters.

"I'm trying," I say quietly. "Sometimes I still think it's all a dream, and I'll wake up back at Marchette." I shudder a little, and he wraps a burly arm around me. I have never felt so safe as I do now, with Joseph's kind strength encircling me.

When Raoul keeps chattering anxiously, I take him by the hand and lead him into Erik's bedroom. I settle him on the bed with the books, and Joseph brings him a strong-smelling drink. "Take it all," he says. "It will help you sleep."

"Yes, I think I need sleep," says Raoul, ruffling his auburn hair. "I'm sorry I'm not more adaptable to all this. More flexible."

"I'm sure you're flexible enough," says Joseph with a wink. "And you're among friends, however strange they may be. Rest."

He and I leave Raoul to settle himself and sort out his thoughts. We sit on the furs and rugs beside Matthieu's couch and we watch his lovely face, so peaceful in sleep.

Somehow Joseph and I end up scooting nearer to each other, and he reaches up to stroke my cheek with the backs of his fingers.

"You didn't listen to me," he says. "You didn't run from this."

"No."

"And Erik—" he glances aside, his jaw working. "He did not force you or manipulate you?"

"Perhaps a little manipulation. But the choice was mine."

Joseph sighs, relieved. "I love him, but he has a dark side."

"A very dark side. But I like it." I smother a giggle. "Has he ever tied you up with many knots?"

Joseph's eyebrows lift. "He did that to you?"

"He was angry with me because I took off his mask without his permission."

"Ah." Joseph nods. "Erik likes to 'punish' us sometimes. We rather look forward to it, because it usually yields very intense orgasms." He bites his lip and reaches down to adjust his pants.

I scoot a bit nearer to him, letting a question shine through my eyes.

Joseph exhales slowly, his brown eyes lighting in response. He spreads his long legs out in a wide V, and I move between them, placing my legs over his thighs and pulling myself in close, until we are face to face, my center aligned with his. The space between his groin and mine seems flooded with magnetic heat, pulling my pussy toward his cock.

I lift my face to Joseph's, admiring the play of the lamplight on his rich brown skin. His eyes are liquid and deep. His mouth floats over mine, softly brushing my lips.

My entire body is alive, delicately illuminated by his presence. Another moment we refrain, testing each other's restraint—and then he sweeps a hand behind my neck and drags my mouth to his.

I yield to the wonderful warmth of him, the strength of his arms, the rough press of his fingers at my nape, the delicious taste of his tongue. We kiss open-mouthed, cheeks sucking and surging, tongues tangling like liquid flames writhing together. My hips, my thighs, my entire womb, my soul—all of it kindles with rapturous fire. I want to be against him, in

209

him—I want to meld my flesh with his, to take him inside me.

Gasping, I break away. "Fuck me," I breathe.

He sweeps my curls back from my forehead. "You know I can't until the appointed time."

I whine in frustration, kissing him again, sighing into his mouth. Then I pull back once more. "But we can both orgasm without your cock going inside me. That's allowed."

His lips curve, mischief sparking in his eyes. "I suppose it is."

18

MATTHIEU

Last thing I knew, I was being beaten senseless, pain exploding through my body everywhere.

Accused of something I would never do. Crushed by the fists and feet of four men, brothers of a woman I never touched.

I thought I was going to die.

But when my eyes open, I feel—sore, yes—but not broken. And right in front of me is the most magnificent sight—the staid and solemn Joseph kissing Christine with such lustful abandon it almost makes me blush. She's releasing tiny soft moans into his mouth, and he's responding with enthusiastic moans of his own, sweeping his large hands up and down her back while she bucks shamelessly against him. They're both clothed, but she's clearly trying to get the friction her pussy needs.

Joseph's eyes open briefly, and his gaze meets mine. Instantly he shifts Christine back a little. "Matthieu?"

She turns, her plump lips damp, her eyes bright. "Oh, Matthieu! How do you feel?"

"Better, now that I have such a lovely view," I say. "Don't stop on my account. In fact, why don't you two strip and proceed from there? I'm sure a little pleasure would help me heal faster."

I reach between my legs, where my cock is growing hard—but my fingers hurt, and my wrist aches. Wincing, I let my arm fall back against the sofa.

Joseph and Christine exchange a conspiratorial look.

"Miss Daaé," he says, in a lofty tone. "It strikes me that this is the perfect occasion for a little tutoring in the art of fellatio."

"Fellatio?" she says, her face falling. "I was hoping to make him come with my mouth."

I chuckle, wheezing a little. "That's what he means, precious. The art of pleasing a man's cock with your mouth. Giving head."

"I'll tell you what to do for Matthieu, and you'll pleasure him," says Joseph.

"Oh, yes." Christine clasps her hands.

"But first, I want you both stripped to your underthings," I tell them. "And you have to do what I say, because I am the poor wounded victim."

Joseph rolls his eyes, but Christine is already disrobing. I laugh, incredulously delighted by how quickly and enthusiastically she's embraced the art of sexual pleasure.

They work together to pull off my pants, and my cock springs upright so eagerly we all chuckle.

"Now, Christine, kneel by the couch and lean in," says Joseph. "There. Rise up on your knees a bit. That way you can take him deeper. First, begin by tasting him however you like. Kiss the head of his cock, lick his shaft, anything."

With her eyes locked on mine, Christine puts out her little pink tongue and touches the tip of my cock with it.

I groan, and my cock bounces. She grins, pleased with herself. She licks me leisurely, from the base of my cock to the head, each wet sweep another layer of erotic torture. Meanwhile Joseph walks around her and begins fondling my nipples.

Faint moans break from me—I can't hold them back.

"Hear that, Christine?" Joseph asks. "I love the sounds he makes."

"Mmm." She's sucking the head of my cock as if it's a candied sweet.

I release a soft mew, writhing a little, and Joseph wickedly plucks my nipple. My hips jerk upward. "God, Joseph," I whine. "Christine—mercy."

"Put him in your mouth now," orders Joseph. "As far as you can go, until his cock head touches the back of your throat. Open your throat like you do when you sing—ah, good girl. That's it."

I'm all the way inside Christine's mouth, her beautiful, perfect mouth. I pant aloud, staring at her lips wrapped around my cock.

"Move your head now. Like this." Joseph takes her head and guides her mouth up and down. "Does that feel good, Matt?"

I whimper—shrill, breathless, incoherent—and he grins. "You sound like a girl when you're aroused, Matthieu. I love it. Work your tongue around his shaft, Christine. Suck on him. Then run him all the way to the back of your throat again—yes."

She gags, and I reach toward her, touching her shoulder. "Don't be sick, precious. Only go as far as you're comfortable."

Christine pulls away, leaving my shaft glossy with her saliva. "You taste so good, Matthieu. I could suck your pretty cock all day."

"Fuck." The word jerks from Joseph. His undershorts are wildly extended. "Christine, lift your ass. I won't go inside, but I have to come on your skin."

She arches her back, pushing her sweet ass out and upward, even as she continues mouthing me. He pulls down her panties and groans at the sight.

"How does her pussy look, Joseph?" I ask. "Describe it to me."

"It's wet," he says.

"How descriptive." I laugh breathlessly. "*Merde*, Christine—I'm going to come."

"Then come," she says, with a lovely smile. "Come in my mouth." She spreads slim, delicate fingers across my abdomen, and my belly tightens at the touch. Her wet lips glide over my cock head again, welcoming me into the sweet suction of her mouth.

Joseph has centered his shaft in the crease of her bottom, and he's pushing himself between her round creamy cheeks, the blunt head of his cock aimed for the small of her back. He's sliding through her ass, she's sucking me off so beautifully—I watch his gorgeous cock throb as he groans, muscles contracting, jetting pearly ropes of cum across her back.

"Fuck!" I scream, and I come hard in Christine's mouth. She accepts it all, sucking and swallowing as if she's enjoying a delicious treat.

19

I am still rocking between Christine's ass cheeks, riding out my orgasm, when I glance up and see Raoul standing in the bedroom doorway, watching the three of us. His cheeks are flushed, his hair rumpled. He looks impossibly pretty in his loose shirtsleeves. Like a normal man, not a noble. Not a Vicomte.

He looks like someone I would fuck.

"So you all do this—often?" he says nervously. But there's raw desire in his eyes.

"This is our first time together, all three of us." Christine rises, wiping her mouth. "It's so much fun, Raoul."

I walk toward him, utterly naked. I know I'm a fine specimen of a man. I enjoy his look of half-guilty admiration.

"Matthieu and I have already come," I say. "But Christine hasn't. That will be your task. Cock up, Chagny, and do your duty."

He stares, mouth parted—but then he presses his lips together and nods firmly. As I thought. This man simply needs to be given a goal, a challenge, and he suddenly becomes an earnest participant.

"Christine, do you want his mouth or his fingers?" I ask.

"I want him to kiss me with his mouth, and pleasure me with his fingers," she says shyly.

In moments they are arranged on the sofa, Raoul reclining with Christine lying against him, her back to his chest, her corset her only bit of clothing.

Raoul leans down, Christine tilts her face up, and they kiss sweetly, tenderly, almost innocently, as if they have both been waiting for each other's lips, and they want to slowly savor these moments. It's so touchingly intimate I can't look at them long, so I wipe Matthieu's cock, pull his pants up, and fetch a cloth and basin so I can wash the blood from his hair.

Eventually Raoul's hand slips between Christine's thighs, and she opens her pussy to him with an ardent sigh. Matthieu and I watch him play with her, leaving most of the direction to Christine, learning what she likes by observation. Raoul devotes himself to her pleasure with a determined intensity and a genuine care that endears him to me even more.

I exchange nods with Matthieu, a silent confirmation that this man is one of us.

Matthieu begins to murmur encouragement. "Yes, precious, yes. His fingers feel so good in your pussy, don't they?"

"Oh yes," she breathes. "Raoul's fingers are so deep in my pussy."

"You're going to come for us, aren't you, pet?" I add, sinking onto the end of the sofa, near her feet. I pick up one of her delicate ankles and kiss her dancer's calluses, pressing my lips to each toe. She inhales raggedly, writhing, and Raoul pumps his fingers faster inside her.

"Come for me, darling," he says. "My friend, my love, my Christine. Come for me—come for us." He swirls his slick thumb over her clit, and her thighs squeeze together around his hand as a shrill note soars from her throat. I let her squirm through the orgasm, but I keep my hold on her ankle.

"Do you feel her pussy clenching around your fingers, Raoul?" croons Matthieu. "That means you did well. Hold her now, soothe her. Beautiful Christine."

Raoul kisses her temple, her cheek, and she sighs against him, blissful tears oozing from the corners of her lashes. When he finally takes his hand out of her, I reach for his wrist, and with my eyes fixed on his, I lick the taste of her from his slender fingers.

"Well done, handsome," I tell him.

Once we have all cleaned our hands and put our clothes back on, I bring out more liquor and food from Erik's stores. We eat, we drink, and then we sleep tumbled against each other—Christine between Matthieu's legs, with her head in the hollow of his hip, and me on the floor, slumped against the sofa, with the Vicomte's head in my lap.

That is how Erik finds us hours later, when he returns. I rouse briefly, setting a finger to my lips so he will not wake the others.

Erik is pale, but he looks triumphant. Which does not bode well for the men who beat Matthieu.

"All of them?" I whisper, and he nods, miming a noose. The smile he gives me is a death's-head grin, a skeletal grin—the grin of a reaper.

Four bodies. I wonder if he concealed them somewhere or strung them up for people to find. Probably the latter.

He put us all at risk by killing them. Still, I can't fault him for it. He defends his own with the passion of a dragon guarding precious treasures. He would do the same for me, for any of us.

And I would kill for him too.

I let him know it with a long, heated look. He hesitates, then walks to me and leans down, kissing me with a mouth that tastes of blood and death. Still, my heart stirs, quickening.

I love him. Whatever he is, whatever he does. I drive my tongue into his mouth so he will know it.

20

Joseph's kiss is an acceptance of me, of what I needed to do to avenge the damage those men did to my sweet Matthieu. Perhaps Joseph would not have kissed me so deeply if he knew that I hung the bodies across the stage, left them dangling purple-faced and swollen-eyed for the managers to see the next morning.

There will be an investigation, of course. But no one will be able to find any clues, or prove anything. I am adept at erasing my tracks, and with my growing influx of new magic, hiding the traces of my crime is even easier than it has previously been.

Still, I decide it is best to give the others some space, since news of what I've done will soon begin to circulate through the Opera House.

I wake Raoul at dawn, remove my mask, and speak to him of dragons and magic. I have pushed him and Christine through this discovery process far more quickly than I did Matthieu and Joseph, and perhaps I may live to regret that. But for now, Raoul seems intrigued enough to keep quiet about my nature, so once I'm convinced of his silence, I send him back to his cold, empty house and his dying parents.

The hangings I perpetrated might be too much for Raoul to accept, but I am confident that the managers will tell him nothing about it. They do not want to scare off their patron.

Matthieu goes back to his mother after another healing session with me. I fuck him before he leaves, rutting deep in his ass, releasing cum and magic inside him so he will have more power if he needs it. He is so hard during the fucking that he shoots cum from his cock without a single touch from his own fingers or mine.

Matthieu does not berate me for killing the men who hurt him. I believe he is grateful.

Joseph does not rebuke me either, though he ends up being one of the men who has to take down the bodies from the stage. Joseph loves Matthieu as much as I do. Perhaps he is secretly delighted with my revenge.

Christine returns to her usual routine—practice and rehearsal. She is now the official understudy for La Carlotta, though I'm sure Carlotta hates it. I did not see Christine's reaction when she found out about the hangings. I dread learning what she thinks of me now. Perhaps I should give her a gift of some kind, to show my affection.

Five days after the hangings, on the night of the next performance of La Guerre, I return to Box 5.

Since I fucked Christine, I have discovered the ability to make myself imperceptible to humans for short time—a sort of camouflage. I ply that new talent when I slip into my box. A good thing, too, because several officers are hiding among the curtains, waiting to snatch the Opera Ghost when he enters. No doubt the managers told the authorities all about their "ghost" and his threats. Those threats are their solitary clue to the perpetrator of the murders.

Entirely concealed from their view, I pluck the envelope containing my salary off the cushioned seat of a chair. This is the bait for the trap, but I am no mouse. I am a predator, and I will not be caught.

I retreat from Box 5, while the officers break out in frantic whispers because the door opened and closed, yet they could see no one.

I smile as I stride away. Everything is proceeding exactly as I wished. My nest of lovers is nearly complete, and we will secure our connection soon, on the night of the masquerade ball. Both Joseph and Matthieu introduced the idea of a masquerade to the theater managers, at separate times and in subtle ways. Moncharmin and Richard seized upon the concept with a desperation born of fear.

A night of wine, sparkling lights, food, and debauchery. Just the sort of thing to drive away a ghost.

Since my place in Box 5 is occupied by the officers, I slink through the shadows backstage and mount the narrow steps and ladder to the catwalk high above. From this towering vantage point, I can see everything on the stage and a swatch of the audience as well, though I am too shrouded in shadow for them to notice me. My camouflage ability is shortlived, so I cannot depend on it for too long. The darkness is my friend, my muse, my mentor, as it has always been.

My hearing, always exceptional, has improved dramatically since I took Christine's virginity. Which in normal circumstances would be a delight, but in the case of La Carlotta's violent butchery of her first aria, it is more pain than pleasure. It is agony, in point of fact. I cannot bear her screeching.

At one point during the dancing, Carlotta veers from her appointed place and bumps into Christine, whom she blames, of course, with a virulent hiss: "Out of my way, you smelly little goat!"

Christine shies from the diva, and my heart roars in her defense.

"A goat, eh?" I murmur. "Let us see who will bleat for mercy."

Curses are tricky things, and they take a substantial amount of power. I have cast them from time to time, when a dancer or a chorus member did not perform to the standards of my Opera House and needed to be let go. Before my magic was fully unlocked, such a curse would render me weak for days.

Now, with my magic unfettered, the curse I perform on Carlotta feels laughably easy. It takes only a few whispered words in the native tongue of the dragons, along with a small burst of my power. As I cast it, I feel a ripple through my body—something shifting involuntarily—a strange sensation over my skin.

Heart pounding, I try to ignore it until the curse is complete. And then, crouched on a beam above the stage, I plunge a hand beneath my cloak, vest, and shirt, seeking the shoulder that is covered in scales.

The scales are still there, but they appear to have spread further across my chest.

My heart jolts. Is it possible that I am finally gaining the ability to shift wholly from human to dragon and back again? I would even settle for being wholly human in form, without any dragon shifting.

But a moment later a crawling sensation creeps over my face, neck, and body, and the patch of scales returns to its usual size and shape.

I have not mastered shifting yet. But those few seconds have given me hope. Perhaps once I fuck Christine's sweet juicy pussy again, once she is linked to all the men in my nest, I will have what I need.

Resigning myself to patience where shifting is concerned, I sit astride the beam and wait for my curse to reveal itself.

And it does, quickly. As Carlotta begins to sing her next lines, she lets out a horrid bleat, like a diseased goat. After coughing and clearing her throat, she tries again. A louder bleat, almost a scream, wrenches from her mouth. She claps her hands over her lips, squawking in confused anguish.

Someone brings her water, and she attempts the lines one more time, with the same result. The crowd, shocked at first, is laughing now, roaring with helpless merriment at her expense.

The curtains are drawn, and Christine is hustled away to put on the costume of the leading character, while Carlotta is helped to her dressing room. And so I spend a delightful two hours reveling in my sweetheart's lovely liquid tones, while I prowl the beams and the catwalk.

Christine outdoes herself, belting notes that make my skin shiver with delight. But there's a plaintive sorrow in her tone that only I can distinguish—I, who taught her everything about her voice.

She is sad, and I think I know why. My innocent lamb is disappointed in me. She knows I killed those men, and it has shaken her faith in her Angel.

Once the performance is over, I retrieve the gift I brought for her from the nook where I concealed it. Then I hurry through the passages in the wall, looking for her through the mirrors in the dressing room and her bedroom. I even peer into the chapel and the girls' shared privy in the dormitory. But she is nowhere to be found.

Desperate, I step through one of the mirrors and stalk the halls in my cloak and cowl until I find

Joseph, still cleaning up backstage. I stand in the shadow of a set piece and beckon to him.

When he comes close, I seize the front of his shirt. "Where is Christine? Have you seen her?"

"No," he says, jerking free. "*Merde*, Erik. What is wrong with you?"

"I am—" I pinch my lips, grinding my jaws together. "I am afraid she despises me now, after what I've done. What if she rejects me? What if she tells the authorities about all of us?"

"She won't," he assures me. "Erik, look at me. It will be all right. I believe she left the stage with Matthieu—if you find him, you may discover where she went."

"And the Vicomte?" I ask. "Have you seen him tonight?"

Joseph smirks. "He is waiting for me in my room. I promised to take him in the ass for the first time, very gently. He is terrified of the size of your cock, and he wants to practice before taking you."

My cock stirs—and my stomach actually ripples with foolish delight. "Raoul wants me to fuck him?"

"He wants it very much, though he can hardly bear to admit it. He was stammering so adorably when he voiced his request to me. I got hard just watching him blush and stumble over the words."

"See that you please him well," I instruct. "Use the bottle of lubricant I gave you to ease the way. And a little magic to take the edge off any pain. And do not forget to tend to his cock while you're fucking him."

"I know, I know." Joseph nods and brushes his lips to my cheek. "Good luck with Christine, my love."

CHRISTINE

The roof of the Opera House is a stark place of cold stone pavers and colder statues. Stagnant rainwater pools in a few recesses, and moss grows in the cracks of a great rearing centaur. I peer beneath the centaur and see that the sculptor gave it a cock—an enormous one of ridiculous length, tucked tight against its belly. Naughty artist, to include such details up here, where few would see them.

Setting down my lantern, I pull my cape tighter around myself as the icy wind whips me.

I came up here for clarity. To think about the man who entered my body, promised me his devotion and protection, claimed me for himself.

What kind of man would hang four people across the Opera stage?

The act matches what little I've been told of dragons and their impetuous, selfish cruelty. Perhaps I did wrong, flinging myself so wholeheartedly into this den of desire, into this dragon's hoard of souls and bodies. Perhaps he considers me one more treasure to claim, one more tool for his pleasure and power. Nothing more.

It was strange, the way Carlotta's voice acted tonight. I wonder if Erik had anything to do with it. He did promise me I would have the leading role again, that he would ensure it.

Strange, malevolent man, dangerous and beautiful.

"Christine, Christine."

The male voice is a golden melody, slithering through the cold of the night and winding around me, warming me.

I can't see him yet, but he is somewhere on this roof.

A red rose drops at my feet.

"You did well tonight, my prima donna," he croons. "I am pleased with you, little lamb. But I fear you are displeased with your Angel."

It's tempting to slip into the role of the innocent with him. But I don't use the sweet, girlish voice I employ when we're playing that game. I use another tone of mine—a stronger one. The voice of the new, more confident Christine.

"No more games, Erik," I say. "Come here. I need to speak with you."

His broad-shouldered silhouette emerges from the shadows. "You're instructing me now?"

"You murdered four men."

"Because they beat Matthieu until he was nearly dead. If I didn't have magic, he would have died."

"And the threat to his life justifies the taking of four other lives?"

"I had to do it. They needed to pay for what they did, and the killing served a dual purpose—reminding those fuckwit managers who is really in charge of this Opera House."

I'm trembling a little, from cold and from the vehemence with which he speaks; but I don't give in. "You think you're a god, don't you? Superior to everyone?"

He sets down a paper-wrapped package he's carrying and strides forward, aggression rolling off him in fierce waves. He towers over me, masked and maniacal, his black cloak swirling behind him. "I rule here, Christine. I make the decisions."

"And the men you call lovers are afraid of you. They fear you and they adore you, just as they fear and crave your punishments. I doubt Matthieu ever challenges you, but I know Joseph does. You need that, Erik, or you will become the kind of dragon in the terrible stories. A wretched, brutal monster."

He reaches for me so quickly I startle, stumbling back, my hands flying up in defense. A pulse of energy thrums through the air between us, and Erik flies backward, crashing to the pavers several paces away.

I stare at my hands, shocked.

He scrambles to his feet, eyes bright with interest. "I wasn't going to hurt you, Christine."

"I—what happened?"

"You used raw magical energy. It can be emitted from your body in various ways, or directed with charms and spells."

"I thought you said it would take several trysts with you before I gathered enough magic to use."

"Perhaps I was wrong in my interpretation of the texts. Or perhaps you are more receptive to magic than I thought." He approaches cautiously, raising his eyebrows for my permission. I nod, and he takes my hands, inspecting them. Then he lifts my skirts unceremoniously and checks the skin on my belly where he marked his sign.

"It's glowing," he says. "Look."

I peer over the skirts that he's holding bunched against my chest. The lines he drew, usually invisible, are gleaming faintly red.

He touches the sign reverently. "You and I are linked," he murmurs.

"Like you and the boys are?"

"This is different." He lets my skirts fall. "*You* are different. I've seduced women before, but only for a night's pleasure. You are the first one I've pursued for something more—the first one I—" He turns away, so all I can see is the masked side of his face. His hands clench at his sides.

I wait.

After a moment, he says, "I thought my relationship with you would be like the ones I have with Joseph and Matthieu. But you, Christine—you're more fragile, and yet more resilient. You are deeply gullible, foolishly naïve, far too prone to obsess over the latest new thing to cross your path—and yet I find myself craving your faults as deeply as I admire your strengths. You are clever, kind, and courageous, as Matthieu and Joseph are, but you are a woman. I cannot treat you the same way I treat them."

I drift toward him, because he looks so very alone. My fingers creep over his, loosening his fist, slipping into the heated center of his palm.

He turns swiftly to face me, and his eyes are full of sweet, pained affection. "I want to give you something."

With a squeeze of my hand he pulls away and fetches the paper-wrapped package. "Normally such an instrument should not be up here, in such temperatures, but I laid a little magic on it to keep it warm."

From the wrapping he lifts a violin—glossy red-brown wood, beautifully crafted. There's a bow, too, strung with white horsehair.

"I purchased this violin at an auction a few years ago," he says. "One of several times I've had to emerge to do business beyond the Opera House. It was made by a great craftsman who was also a fantastic musician in his own right." He turns over the instrument and shows me a tiny "G.D." with a swirl, carved into the wood.

Gustave Daaé.

"My father made this violin," I breathe.

"He did. It is the only violin I own, my most prized possession besides my organ and my book collection, both of which are too large to give you, though you may use them anytime." He laughs a little, almost as if he is nervous. "This violin is yours now, Christine."

Tears begin to pool in my eyes. "Angel."

He shakes his head. "Not an angel, or a god. I am flawed, I know it. I rule harshly because Matthieu and Joseph need someone strong, a leader. They depend on me. Yet sometimes I dominate when I should sympathize. I blame them when I should be looking at my own faults. I am a natural conqueror, Christine. It is part of my instinct to rule, to suppress, to collect and control. I refuse to be weak, pliant, and submissive—with one exception."

He's sinking to his knees, holding up the violin. "My terror of losing your heart overwhelms everything else. I did not realize how much I wanted all of you until this night. Not only your darling pussy or your clever mind, but your *heart*, little lamb. Your soul. Your love. Those must be mine as well. And to earn them, I will yield to you in anything. I love you."

He bows his head, black waves tumbling around his temples.

My heart is too full to reply. But I reach out, and I take the violin and the bow. "I do not know how to play."

He looks up, smiling. "I can teach you. Did you know, Christine, that the members of a dragon's nest retain their youth far longer than other humans do? And they live for many more decades than the average human, as long as their dragon remains alive and their sexual bond stays strong. You will have plenty of time to learn any skill you want."

"So if we all keep fucking, we get to be young for decades and enjoy a far longer lifespan? Have you told Raoul this?"

"I have. I could tell he was beginning to lose his mind with all the information, so I thought he should know of the additional benefits. I'm fairly sure the promise of youth and long life won him over."

"I did wonder how he accepted it all so easily," I say.

"That, and I told him my future goals and plans," Erik admits.

"The secret plans you wouldn't trust me with?" I frown at him.

"Raoul is a man who needs purpose right now. He needs to know that he matters, that he can effect lasting change with the power and riches that are his. He is watching his parents grow old, Christine, and it has made him fear his own mortality. I gave him what he needed so that he could see his way clear to join us, wholeheartedly. And I had to do it quickly, because of the circumstances. He could not be allowed to leave my lair, knowing what he knew, unless I could be sure of him."

My brows draw together more tightly. It feels like Erik knows Raoul better than I do, though he has spent less time with him. Erik has a talent for perceiving exactly what aches inside someone, and then soothing that pain.

Erik touches my forehead, smoothing away my frown. "If it helps, I would have killed him if I wasn't convinced of his trustworthiness."

I gape at him. "How is that helpful?"

"Him, I would have killed easily—with regrets, yes, but I could have borne it. You, I would have trapped in my lair forever. If you could not be trusted, I would have kept you prisoner, no matter how bothersome you became. I would never have the heart to end you."

"You twisted bastard," I whisper, clutching the bow and violin in one hand, drawing his face down to mine with the other. He's right—I'm oddly flattered that he wouldn't have been able to kill me.

"I will tell you everything I told Raoul," Erik says. "I swear. But first, dance with me."

"There's no music."

"Ah. Wait a moment. If I could borrow this." He takes the violin from me and plays a lovely, lilting melody with sweeping lines and soaring notes. When he sets the violin down in its wrapping again, the song continues to play, over and over, the music spiraling around us as he takes both my hands.

"You're using magic to keep the music playing," I murmur wonderingly.

"A little trick I've perfected. Come, my lamb."

We waltz together on the rooftop, through the scattered scarlet leaves, by the light of my lantern and the bright, cold stars. Erik begins to sing to me, softly, weaving his voice with the delicate music. He coaxes me to sing with him, so I harmonize until he pauses.

"That phrase would sound delightful if you could hit an E6." There's a challenge sparkling in his yellow eyes.

"I can't," I protest. "Not yet."

"Oh, you can. Come now, let us practice. Sit here." He lifts me and sets me on the pedestal of the great centaur statue, right between its front legs. He kisses my mouth and shoves my skirts up around my waist.

"Erik!" I gasp.

"Hush, little lamb. There is no one to see." With a short knife from his boot, he proceeds to cut away my panties. Cold air whispers across my sex.

"Interesting that you chose this statue," I say, breathless. "Did you see its cock?"

"I designed these statues. Sculpted them myself and sold them to the Opera House."

My jaw drops. "You did?"

"It was my first arrangement with the former Opera House manager, Mercier. I also invented the message chute system the boys and I use to communicate quickly. And I have laid the marks of my genius upon this place in so many other ways."

"I want to see them all," I tell him.

238

"Sweet Christine, always so earnest and curious." He kneels and breathes warm air onto my naked pussy. "Begin practicing your scales—the ones we usually do."

I begin as directed, following the notes like stairsteps, up and down, then switching higher and repeating the pattern. My breath catches when Erik begins to lick my pussy, but he looks up and frowns. "You falter or miss a single note, and I will stop doing this."

"Don't stop," I plead, and I keep climbing the musical staircase, my voice soaring a little higher each time. Erik is humming against my pussy, swiping his tongue rapidly over my fold. His fingers dip into my soaking slit, delving far inside. Glittering prickles of pleasure circle through my clit, chasing each other inside my belly, vibrating along my thighs. But he won't give my clitoris the full attention it needs.

"Please, Angel," I beg.

"You stopped singing." He glares at me. "Start over."

Once again I begin mounting the notes, and this time I don't stop. I push my voice higher in tandem with the spiraling waves of pleasure. I'm straining to reach the height of ecstasy, the sensual peak to which Erik's tongue and fingers are driving me.

My pussy lips are drenched, and my slit is quivering, verging on bliss.

"You can't come until you sing an E6," Erik says, and presses his lips into my sex again. My back arches—I'm starting to come—I shriek, pure and high, the note he craves. Immediately he suckles my clit while pumping his slick fingers faster, and I explode into glory and thrills, screaming the note again as the orgasm floods my body.

I wonder if the stars heard me come for my Angel.

22

CHRISTINE

The masquerade ball is a whirl of lights and color. The sharp smell of bubbling wine fills the air, and there's a mingled haze of cloying perfumes and colognes.

Erik insisted I arrive with the other dancers, escorted by no one. I belong to my four men for the night, and that secret claim has already slicked my thighs with arousal. I'm wearing no panties, no pantalettes or stockings or garters, by order of the Phantom. Beneath the gorgeous ruffled skirts of my gown, my pussy is bare for the boys. I suspect that tonight is the night when they will all come inside me, though Erik would not say for sure. He would only tell me that he has laid a neutralizing spell on all of them so they cannot get me pregnant.

"The spell will last until the day you ask me to lift it," he said. "As for me, I've sworn to never have children. I am not a full dragon, and I would not condemn them to a fate like mine—stuck between forms, torn between a dragon's nature and the humanly vulnerable side of myself."

"I think you try to forget your humanity sometimes," I told him. "But it's part of what makes you lovable. The tender side, hidden under the savagery and the punishments. Speaking of which, what does a girl have to do to be bound by you again?"

His mouth slants, a wicked grin. "Challenge me and see what you'll get."

So I'm doing one thing tonight that he told me not to do. I'm accepting dances from other men— and there are plenty of them wanting a chance to circle the ballroom with the mysterious ingenue whose performances have been such a success. I suppose my mask isn't much of a disguise—it's a simple one across my eyes, decorated with white lace, feathers, and five-pointed stars made of glittering sequins. People can easily tell who I am.

The men I dance with are masked, but so far I've been able to discern that they're strangers, not one of my lovers. I let my dance partners encircle my waist, lace their fingers with mine, pull me close against their bodies. My breasts are on full display in this gown; the neckline barely covers my nipples, and most of the men seem entranced by my cleavage. That will surely infuriate Erik. I only hope he does not decide to strangle every man in the place.

La Carlotta is at the masquerade too, in a bejeweled porcelain mask and hoop skirts so wide people have to crowd away from her when she passes. Piangi is at her elbow, pompous as ever, wearing a red-faced cherublike mask with a stiff halo that nods as he walks.

Carlotta eyes me constantly, a perpetual sneer on her face. It's unnerving. Her stare and the heat of the room begin to oppress me. I do believe Carlotta has directed the ushers not to serve me, because whenever I try to get a drink or a bit of refreshment, the person with the tray heads in the opposite direction.

"Would you get me some water?" I ask my partner, a rotund gentleman who has kept his hands in respectable places during our dance.

He bobs a bow and hurries away.

Immediately a long-legged figure in a beautifully enameled fox mask takes his place, sweeping me into the next dance.

"Excuse me," I object. "I'm still with that gentleman over there. He merely left to fetch me a drink."

The fox twirls me roughly and pushes me into the arms of a silver-masked wolf.

"Wait," I gasp. "What are you—"

The wolf jerks me against his body, cupping my ass boldly, while the fox slinks around us. Another figure with a lion's head moves in, stealing me, grinding his body against mine.

They're working me toward the edge of the grand hall, toward a side corridor that leads to a few private parlors. And in the opening of that corridor stands a figure in a scarlet cloak, with the mask of a crimson dragon.

The three predators herd me toward him while the dance music from the main hall echoes around us. My heart is thundering like the beat of the orchestra drums. I am a violin, tense and ready for my master's touch—a clarinet awaiting the breath of its owner. I am the lustful throbbing drone of the cello and the shrill orgasmic trill of the flute.

The red dragon hands me a glass of champagne, and I sip a little quickly before his gloved hand closes on my arm, hustling me down the corridor. The urns along the hall have been stuffed with hothouse blooms, and their rich fragrance suffuses the air. Flames gutter gently in candelabra, disturbed by our passage.

The red dragon flings open a pair of doors, while the fox, wolf, and lion encircle me, pressing me into the room beyond. This space is candlelit as well, but there are no flowers here—only a few cushioned sofas and a low table. One of the sofas has several extra cushions piled on it, with furs draped over the back.

The doors of the room stand ajar, and distant music drifts in from the gala. The four masked figures begin to move around me, to dance, catching my hands and whirling me with them. I try to guess who is who from their heights, but some of them are wearing heeled boots, and the full-headed masks do not provide me with any hints of features or hair color.

I am to be rutted by four masked men.

What if they are not who I think they are?

Experimentally I snap my hands outward, letting my anxiety flow like I did on the rooftop—and two of the men stumble back, struck by the pulse of magical energy. One of them says, *"Merde,"* in Matthieu's voice, and another says "Hush!"

I grin, reassured. That burst of magic wasn't as strong as what I used on Erik. Perhaps the power I gathered from him is fading, and I need more.

The silver wolf steps in suddenly, pushing down the neckline of my gown, and my breasts pop out, round and full, nipples tight with arousal. The wolf shifts to stand behind me, reaching around to cup my breasts, squishing them in his gloved hands, bumping his erection against my backside. I gasp as my nipples are manipulated and massaged in the most lecherous way.

The fox and the lion move in next, seizing my arms and pulling me behind the sofa that's draped in furs. They bend me over the sofa back, so that my ass is pushed out and my breasts hang down above the seat cushions.

The doors to this room are still partly open. I'm facing the hall, bare-breasted, as two guests stroll past. They do not glance my way.

I'm trembling, my arousal trickling along my thighs. My face is a roaring flame, and my pulse throbs in my clit.

Gloved hands push my gown up. Bunch it around my waist.

Someone smacks my ass cheek, and the sting immediately generates a responsive tingle in my pussy.

Hands urge my legs wider apart, gloved fingers stroking my thighs, prodding lightly at the fleshy lips between my legs. My pussy is entirely on display, spread open and weeping with lust.

Something presses between my folds, nudging deeper. A hard, hot length.

A cock.

There's a cock inside me. I have no idea whose it is, and somehow that makes me even more desperate to be fucked.

The cock rushes in deeper, and I gasp. It withdraws partway, then plunges into me again, flexing compulsively inside my pussy. Then it slips out, leaving the lips of my sex wet and trembling.

Whoever it was abandoned my pussy without cumming.

What are they doing?

Another cock shoves inside me, pumping twice quickly. A soft male groan—I don't know who made the sound.

That cock is gone, but another takes its place, dipping in, dragging solid and thick through my sex. I think it's Erik, but he disappears before I can be sure.

The fourth cock sweeps my arousal along the seam of my sex before thrusting firmly, fucking me three times.

Then I'm empty again, and I whine in protest.

I'm being lifted off the sofa back. The lion and the fox are unlacing my dress, pulling it off me. They strip me bare and I stand before all of them, my sex leaking down my legs, my face red, my mouth and pussy lips swollen with desire. My breasts feel full and tight and warm.

Their cocks protrude from their pants, all mutely begging to be sucked and fucked.

The red dragon hands me a note that says, "Guess who we are correctly and you get cock."

I inspect him carefully. "This isn't really fair to you, Joseph, since yours is a different color."

The dragon removes his mask, and it's Joseph, grinning. "I fooled you at first, though. You thought I was Erik."

"I did." I step closer, eyeing the male organs before me. Strange that I was so shy of inspecting a statue's equipment when I first arrived, and now I'm guessing the identity of my lovers by their cocks.

"This game is easy." I point to the thickest cock, the one with the snaking vein and the bulging head. "Erik."

He removes the wolf mask. He's wearing his usual white mask beneath it. "Correct, little lamb."

"And now—" I've sucked Matthieu's cock, and I recognize it at once—slim and lovely like its owner.

"Matthieu." I dab the precum from the tip of his penis, and when he removes his fox mask I lick his wetness from my finger. His green eyes flame hotter with lust. His tongue slips along the seam of his mouth, and the little gold ring rolls so temptingly against his plump lip that I lean forward to kiss him.

But Erik stops me.

"Last one," he says.

I reach out, circling Raoul's penis with my fingers. I remember it from the courtyard, when Erik rubbed their two cocks to climax. His member is a good length, solid, well-formed. He groans as I touch him.

"Sweet Raoul," I murmur. "My old friend."

He takes the lion mask off and shakes out his auburn waves. He's blushing deeply, and his gaze seems magnetized by my bare breasts.

"May I have cock now?" I ask Erik.

"Get on the sofa, there." He points to the one with extra cushions. "Legs as wide as you can get them. Sit on the pillows so we don't have to crouch to access your hole. And tilt your pelvis up."

I arrange myself with several cushions under my bottom and one at my lower back. My whole skin is humming, burning—my clit is so sensitive that I whimper when a bit of cushion fabric brushes it while I settle in.

"Joseph." Erik nods to him. "You decide who comes inside her first."

"Matthieu," says Joseph immediately.

"Are you serious?" Matthieu sounds touched and delighted. "You would do that for me, Joseph?"

"You are always giving of yourself to me and Erik," Joseph says gruffly. "Go on. Fuck her."

Raoul steps over and closes the parlor doors, for which I'm grateful. He doesn't lock them, though. We could still be interrupted.

Matthieu is shucking off his clothes. He comes to me, bare and beautiful, green eyes and golden hair. The laughing dancer who welcomed me on my first day.

He kisses me softly, tasting of vanilla and sugar and wine—and then he braces himself against the sofa and puts his pretty cock inside me. I watch it slip between my pink lips. When he pulls out a little, the shaft is gleaming wet. He throws back his head and groans. "Fuck, you feel so good."

23

MATTHIEU

I've never fucked anyone like Christine, and I've fucked around a lot. There is something special about the silken heat of her pussy, the way her large, lovely eyes shine at me, so innocent yet so wicked. She envelops me, her pussy compressing my whole length gently. At the top of her sex is the little nub of flesh and delicate nerves that will send her to heaven. I massage it lightly, and her inner walls spasm around my cock. She's close, but she hasn't arrived. Since Joseph was kind enough to let me go first, I will prepare her for him, but I won't make her come yet. He should have that joy.

Joseph comes up behind me and cups my bare ass with his big, warm hands, while his penis bumps between my cheeks, not invading, just a hint of tender lust. Ecstasy races along my cock and I pump faster, fucking Christine while the other men watch. An explosion of pleasure shoots through my body, and I come hard, whimpering while Christine pulls my mouth to hers.

The sensation that follows is more than sexual. It's a feeling of belonging, a soothing balm to my heart. I am accepted. I am part of something—a family. These people love me. They are proud of me. They will take care of me.

It's all I've ever wanted.

24

CHRISTINE

Matthieu's cum pools in my belly, warm and wonderful. I can feel him twitching inside me. He releases shrill little gasps across my tongue as we kiss.

"You precious darling," I whisper. "I love you."

"I love you, too," he breathes.

A sense of sweet calm washes through me, bathing my soul.

Another firm kiss, a sweep of his tongue through my mouth, and Matthieu is sliding out of me. He plants a quick kiss on Joseph's mouth before collapsing into a chair.

Joseph moves in, still wearing the shirt from his costume, but it's unbuttoned, revealing the powerful slopes of his chest and his beautiful abdominals. He's naked from the waist down, his cock swinging thick and ready.

I squeeze my own breast lightly and bite my lip, looking up at him playfully from under my lashes.

He chuckles. "You were never a virgin at heart, were you?"

I put my tongue out, and he leans in, sucking it briefly before murmuring, "Ready to take my cock, Christine?"

"I've been ready since I met you." I spread my thighs a little wider.

He moves himself into position, but he touches me first, swirling his finger through the lips of my sex. "Your pussy is sloppy with Matthieu's cum," he groans, and his cock twitches. Then he's plunging in, hard and fast.

25

JOSEPH

I fuck Christine like a desperate man, and perhaps I am. Desperate to secure my forever home with these men, this woman. Desperate to complete the bond. I've had hollows in my heart for so long, and each one of my partners fills a different one of those empty places perfectly.

Christine—intelligent, talented, kind-hearted, naïve yet seductively sinful. Erik—passionate, ingenious, dangerous, and as desperate for love as I am. Raoul—a wandering soul, watching his family slip away from him, aching for purpose and place. And Matthieu—cocky, laughing, yet perhaps even more vulnerable than the rest of us, with that sensitive heart of his.

I love them all.

So I rut hard into Christine, and I look her in the eyes. Her breasts are jouncing and jiggling with the force of my thrusts, and her eyes are glazing over. Her lips part as I strike that pleasure-spot deep inside her. She's close to orgasm.

"I love you, you fucking beautiful woman," I say.

Her spine arches, and she comes apart around me. I feel every exquisite flutter of her sex as she clenches on my cock. With a low bellow, I come inside her.

My balls heave and throb, releasing everything I have into her body. As the pulsing pleasure fades, I have an overwhelming sense of being purged, washed, and at peace.

26

Christine's sex is still quaking from the explosive orgasm Joseph gave her. Fuck. I love the sight of a woman in orgasm. The cum pumps out of her in creamy rivulets, trailing through the crease of her bottom, painting her tiny asshole in milky white.

I tear my gaze away from the beautiful sight to see if anyone else is enjoying it, too. Matthieu has pulled a naked Raoul onto his lap, and he's tweaking the Vicomte's nipples to watch his cock jerk. It's a good thing they're bonding. We need Raoul to feel comfortable with all of us.

But Joseph is still watching Christine's pussy, watching her breasts heave. Her cheeks are rosy with pleasure, her mouth red.

I reach over and grip his hand. "She's beautiful, isn't she, our lamb?"

"Yes," he says. "And so are you."

He reaches for my shirt, as if he plans to unbutton it, but I pull away and shake my head. "Not yet. I'm not ready."

He and Matthieu have seen me both unmasked and entirely naked, but I am still uncertain about revealing my whole body to Christine.

I could not bear it if she thinks I'm too monstrous, too detestable.

My cock is already out, so hard it's nearly painful. Thanks to my virile dragon nature, my balls are full to bursting. I will be pouring a river into the lovely body before me.

"Look at this messy little pussy. I'm going to fuck Joseph's and Matthieu's cum back into you," I tell Christine, crawling over her, my lips floating against hers. I take her plump lip in my teeth and bite gently before kissing her.

"Please fill me with cum, Angel," she whispers back.

Groaning, I drag the wide head of my cock up her sex, scooping the dribbling cum and pushing it back inside her. Gripping the back of the sofa on either side of her head, I plunge in, violent bellows breaking from me as I fuck, and fuck, and fuck her. My heavy balls smack against her ass every time I ram inside, and the mating sign on her belly glows red.

27

CHRISTINE

Erik's guttural moans are the sweetest music I've heard all night. Even Matthieu and Raoul stop kissing each other long enough to listen to him fuck me. My sex is so sloppy that each thrust squelches, loud and wet.

I am going to come again. I can feel the orgasm building at the base of my spine, tingles circling between my hips. Erik's arms are braced on either side of me, hard bulging muscle under his shirt, and I use those arms as anchors while my body climbs, climbs, higher, higher—

"I need—" I sob, tossing my head back and forth, "I need, I need—"

"Me," he growls, grinding deeper. "You need *me*, Christine. Fuck. God-fucking-damn you, you feel fucking amazing. Give me everything, your pussy, your soul—tell me you love me! Tell me!"

"I love you!" I scream. "Fuck me harder, please, oh please—"

"You *will* come for me." He's slamming into me now, shaking the entire couch. My whole world is his chest, his rock-hard arms, the pummeling force of his massive cock. I take one hand off his arm and frantically rub my clit, shrieking breathlessly as finally, finally—

"Come for me, Christine!" he cries. "Come for me!"

And I do. I come for him, and wetness squirts from my pussy, bathing his cock, sprinkling the sofa cushions.

I'm screaming, kicking, bucking. I've never felt anything like this.

Raoul is there, on my right, his naked body soothing mine. Matthieu crawls in on my left. And Joseph is holding Erik while he roars and shakes, gushing cum into me. Sweat films Erik's forehead, and his black hair an unruly mess framing his beautiful sharp face, his gorgeous inhuman face. His mask is still in place, but through the wild dazzle of my orgasm I know that he and I have unlocked something, dismantled a wall between us.

As if drawn by the same impulse, he lunges toward me just as I lean toward him. Our mouths crash together, while our bodies keep throbbing, swirling, settling.

"I felt that," Matthieu whispers. "Like a current of energy through my body. Anyone else?"

Joseph nods, and so does Raoul.

"Just one more to complete the nest." Joseph reaches over and grips Raoul's shoulder. "Time to fuck your childhood sweetheart, Vicomte."

When Erik pulls out of me, a flood of cum pours from my sex. This couch is thoroughly wrecked, soaked and sprayed, not to mention nearly torn apart by Erik's powerful arms.

Erik is still unsteady from his violent release, but he takes a moment to cup Raoul's delicate face and kiss him, slow and deep. "Fuck her well," he says, and steps aside.

Of them all, Raoul is the only one who truly understands where I come from, how structured and strict my life used to be. He knew me as the prim, proper, neatly dressed girl who behaved decorously in public and laughed secretly at his jokes; the one who whispered dark fairytales to him when we were supposed to be discussing banal topics like the weather or current events.

He knew me as my former self. So when he moves in between my legs, as I lie wide open and dripping with the cum of three men, I feel a little tentative and unsure.

"Can you take me as I am, and not as I was?" I murmur.

His blue eyes meet mine. "I loved you then innocently. And I love you now, with a fuller understanding of who you are, and who I am. I have always loved you, Christine. And I always will. I commit myself to this—to all of you—" he glances around at the others. "To pleasure your bodies, fulfill your desires. To further your cause, to ensure your safety, to protect and provide for you. To submit myself to the will of our Angel, and to be lover and friend to every man and woman in this room. This is my new purpose."

The light in his face fills my whole being with joy.

"So well-spoken." Matthieu pretends to swoon, and Joseph chuckles. But Erik takes Raoul by the nape of the neck and plants another hard kiss on his mouth. When he pulls away, his yellow eyes glitter with tears.

Then Raoul, Vicomte de Chagny, nudges his cock into my pussy.

28

RAOUL

Christine is slippery, soaked with the release of the other three men, and somehow that makes my whole body harder.

I have reservations in my mind—doubts and guilt, but their voices are growing fainter. The quieter they get, the happier I am.

I'm not indulging my lust without reason. This group is exactly what I needed, though I did not know it until now. With them, I can have the woman I've always loved, and I can fuck men as I've secretly wanted to for years. I can admit the cravings now, accept them, embrace them.

I pump into Christine, slow and gentle. She's had two rough fuckings, and her sex is vibrantly pink and swollen, so I take my time with her, massaging her clit, fondling her breasts—making love to her, soothing her with my cock.

The other men are entwined at the end of the couch, watching and resting. But I barely notice them, because Christine is looking at me with tears in her eyes—sweet, joyful tears.

"I love you, Raoul," she tells me.

I respond with more careful attention to her clit, copying the things I learned from the other night, when I touched her pussy for the first time, when I learned about dragons and struggled to cope with it all.

Since then, I've been reading everything I can find on the subject, and I've learned far more about the Dragon Wars than I ever knew. There was evil, injustice, and misunderstanding on both sides, but the dragons and the mages got the worst of it. Slaughtered. Hunted. Maimed and tortured. Executed.

I want to help Erik. I believe him when he says that not all the dragons were cruel and not all the mages were wicked. Joseph and Matthieu are mages, or they will be, and Christine has an affinity for magic as well. Erik hasn't come inside me yet, but when he does, it's possible I'll find out that I have magical potential too.

I draw my thoughts back to the moment, to Christine's lovely naked body. The curve of her lithe waist, her little dancer's feet, her slim legs, her elegant neck, and her perfect, plump breasts—all of her sings to my passion. My abdomen begins to tighten with impending release.

I'm fucking her, like in the fantasy in Box 5. Fucking her within full view of others. I can't believe this is happening. I feel powerful, joyful, beautiful. My cock flames, throbs—I gasp, and I'm coming. My cum is mingled with that of Joseph, Matthieu, and Erik—my new lovers.

Bliss rushes over my body, raising goosebumps on my skin. I throw my head back and moan softly. To my surprise, Christine echoes me with a quiet cry of her own, and her inner walls ripple around my cock. She came for me, sweet wanton thing that she is. A mellow, lovely orgasm that milks the rest of my release from my balls.

I know this is where she belongs. This makes her happy—this, and the Opera. I could never take either of them away from her. I feel selfish for ever having considered it.

29

I can feel the change in me.

Not just the sated feeling in my balls and belly, not just the soothing influence of the bond we solidified, but a fresh influx of power. Magic flowed out of me into Christine, but the act of fucking her was significant for me as well. She's the one whose virgin pussy unlocked my power, the one I marked as uniquely mine, even though I share her with the others.

I'm roiling with energy, bursting with it. I need to release it somehow, and the best place to do that is down below, in my lair.

"I need to go," I snap.

They all glance at me, startled. Raoul is wiping the cum from Christine's pussy, helping her clean up.

"Why the hurry, dragon?" Joseph's voice is still smoky from sex.

"I feel—" I fumble with the buttons of my pants, my fingers trembling. "I feel—something is happening. I'm changing, inside."

"I feel like I've changed too," Raoul pipes up, but I snarl, "No. Not like that. This is different."

Matthieu steps in, fastening my pants for me, looking up at me with anxious green eyes full of love. "Tell me how to help you."

"I need to get to the lair," I say hoarsely.

"We'll come with you." Christine leaps up, cum running down her inner thigh. Raoul helps her into her dress, and the others dress quickly as well.

I don't want to wait for them. I feel an impending cataclysm that I can't hold off much longer.

But they seem so eager to stay with me, so I wait those few minutes, allowing them to dress and put on their masks. I don mine as well, transforming into the wolf again.

We leave the soiled couch. With so many revelers here, we're certainly not the only ones involved in licentious acts. No one will know it was our group that stained the cushions with cum, sweat, and liquid arousal.

Together we hurry down the hall. "It's fastest to cut through the lobby and the theater," says Joseph. "We can go straight through the backstage area and get to a tunnel that leads to the lair."

I can't reply. I can only follow him, while my bones groan and my nerves burn. There's a fire building inside me, a monster swelling, roaring to break out.

Dizzy and reeling, half-supported by Raoul and Joseph, I stumble through the lobby. Christine holds open the door to the auditorium, her face white and anxious. "Was it something I did?" she whispers.

No, sweet one, I want to say. *It's my wretched dual nature, coming out to play.* But I cannot speak. My teeth are lengthening in my mouth, my tongue thickening.

We're halfway down the central aisle. There are some guests scattered among the seats, most of them half-drunk and keening with laughter, others deeply engrossed in kissing or humping. Overhead hangs the great chandelier, lit with a thousand candles.

Those tiny flickering flames seem to fill my sight, growing larger and larger until they are a vast furnace of billowing flame.

My bones shift, sliding against each other, stretching and expanding, bursting—

I can't make it to the lair—

Christine and the men are flung back as I explode into my new form.

Wings erupt from my shoulders. I am larger than I've ever been—a writhing, coiling shape covered in dark-green scales, with oddly jointed legs and sharp claws. A tail whips behind me, smashing a few theater seats.

Fire burns overhead, blazing, incandescent. I need to be near it.

My new body compacts and then springs upward, huge muscles driving my wings. Flight is as easy and natural as breathing.

270

Below me, people are screaming.

Heedless of their panic, I fly upward to the chandelier, alighting upon it with a crunch of breaking glass. Shards sprinkle the red-carpeted aisle below.

The candle flames brush my scales. Their searing heat is just what I need. I draw the fire into myself, feeding my inner flame, until I have sucked the light from every candle. The theater is much darker now, uplit only by the sconces near the exits and a few footlights along the edge of the stage, in front of the heavy curtains.

Up here in the shadows, I am concealed by the friendly dark. My mind is a whirl of smoke, jagged mirror fragments of myself flashing through my thoughts. What is happening to me? I try to grasp the reality of who I am, what I should do—but I cannot. I am losing myself, I am lost—

The chandelier jerks suddenly, tilting. My weight is too much for it.

Before I can leap off it and take to the air again, the cable holding it rips free of the ceiling and the entire chandelier crashes down onto the seats below.

Pain spears through me in several places. I try to crawl free of the wreckage. It's too dark, too confusing. I cannot find my magic. I cannot understand what is happening.

A soft, sweet voice in the dark, singing a melody I should know. I cling to that song, wrapping my consciousness around it, letting it clarify my thoughts.

I am Erik. Opera Ghost. Dragon and human, stuck between the two—but no longer, because I have completed my first shift into full dragon form.

In the middle of the theater.

Fuck.

Suddenly I sense it again—the tendrils, the frayed threads of my magic, leading into a vast tapestry of power. I follow those threads, latch onto my power, and focus every conscious thought on reverting to my usual form.

The change back to my human shape is just as quick and startling as my switch to dragon form. I have never been so happy to feel my skin, even the scales along my shoulder and face. I try to push further, to eradicate those scales and find a perfect human aspect—but I can't. I suppose I will never be able to look fully human.

Not that it matters now. I have ruined everything.

Someone is sweeping a cloak around my body. I'm caught up in muscled arms—the scent of paint and baked bread—my Joseph. He carries me between two rows of seats, hurries backstage.

"You two take him below," Joseph orders. "Raoul and I need to manage this catastrophe."

Matthieu and Christine move in, supporting me on either side. They help me through the tunnels, and Matthieu poles the boat along the canal while Christine cradles my head in her lap, soothing me with more soft singing.

Vaguely I'm aware that I am being put to bed and covered up. And then my mind gives way to darkness.

When I wake, Joseph is there, sitting in a chair by my bed. His face is solemn.

I let a few tears slide down my cheeks, because I have failed him. Failed them all. I turned into a dragon in the middle of the Opera House, and that event spells death and destruction for our family.

"I am sorry, my love," I whisper. "I have wrecked everything."

"No," he says, gripping my hand. "No, Erik. You did not wreck it all. Raoul and I worked together. We managed things."

My gaze follows his to where Raoul stands on the opposite side of my bed, looking very pleased with himself.

"What do you mean, you managed things?" I press a hand to my forehead. "How?"

"I concocted an alternate truth while I was carrying you to safety, and the moment I turned you over to Christine and Matthieu, I began executing my plan," Joseph says. "And while you've been sleeping through the night and half the day, we spread the cover story throughout the Opera House and into the city. Most of the people who saw you as a dragon were drunk or distracted. And once you sucked the light from the chandelier, it was hard to see you up there. With Raoul's help, I passed around a story that the wine at the masquerade was laced with some new exotic drug."

"We circulated another tale as well," interrupts Raoul eagerly. "We told everyone the managers tried to install a wooden dragon atop the chandelier to amuse the guests and entice more people to see *La Guerre des Dragons*. But the wooden dragon was too heavy, and it brought down the chandelier, you see."

Joseph cuts in. "While everyone was fleeing the theater, I smashed one of the dragon set pieces and scattered the fragments among the chandelier wreckage to corroborate the story. That event, coupled with the rumors of drugged wine, has been quite enough to allay any suspicion of a real dragon."

"And the best news of all," says Raoul, "is that Moncharmin and Richard have resigned as the managers of the Opera House. They left me in sole charge of choosing their replacement. So you see, Erik, this actually works in our favor. It hastens the timeline of your plan quite dramatically." He leans over me, his fine features aglow with excitement. "We are now in charge of l'Opera Lajeunesse. And I have already selected a new manager."

30

 CHRISTINE

I spend most of the day gossiping with the other dancers, perpetuating the false cover story Joseph and Raoul concocted. I'm terribly worried about Erik, but Joseph has assured me that the best way to help him is to ensure no one suspects the presence of a real dragon on the premises.

All performances are canceled indefinitely, of course, and the entire cast is either in the process of leaving out of sheer terror, or thoroughly enjoying the unexpected hiatus. Carlotta and Piangi are long gone.

That evening, I sit disconsolately in my room, wondering if I should try to find my own way down to the lair. I'm nervous about traversing all the secret corridors on my own. What if I get lost in the maze beneath the Opera House?

Idly I practice moving objects without touching them, thanks to my new magical energy. It's entertaining and exciting, but it barely takes the edge off my anxiety.

When Matthieu emerges from my bedroom mirror, I leap up. "How is Erik?"

"He has fully recovered," says Matthieu, wrapping me in a hug. "He went into one of the larger subterranean chambers and practiced shifting for an hour this afternoon. He says he has it under control, that no unexpected shifts will happen again."

"Let's hope not." I drag him toward the mirror. "I want to see him."

When we arrive at the lair, Eric is sitting in an armchair, fully clothed and masked, sipping whisky and smoking with Raoul and Joseph, while Matthieu plays a jaunty tune on the organ.

Erik gives me a wry smile as I race up to him. When I kiss him, his mouth tastes of sweetish smoke and sharp alcohol, with an undercurrent of spicy heat that makes my sex tingle.

"I'm so glad you're all right," I whisper.

"I am better than all right." He kisses me back tenderly. "I am celebrating. My misstep has served us well in the most unexpected way, thanks to the quick thinking of Joseph, the influence of Raoul, and the gossip-mongering of you and Matthieu." He grins at me, a more jubilant and genuine smile than I've ever seen from him. "Are you ready to hear my plans for the future, Christine?"

"I am." I perch on his knee, assuming my best innocent expression. "Tell me, Angel."

"The managers have yielded," he says proudly. "We have complete control of the Opera House. I shall be the creative genius, the artistic director in the shadows. Christine, you shall be the star of every performance, my voice before the masses. Matthieu, you will take over the male dancers and oversee costuming, too, if you like. Raoul, you will serve as the voice of the arts and the spokesman for magical tolerance among the nobles of the city."

He pauses, glancing at Joseph, who crosses his arms.

"Out with it," Joseph growls. "What shitty role have you assigned me, that you're so reluctant to disclose it?"

Erik smiles wider, his golden eyes flashing. "Raoul and I agree on this. You, Joseph, are the new manager of L'Opera Lajeunesse. You will handle the workings of this place far better than any of the previous managers ever did. I trust no one else to implement my vision."

Joseph swallows, and I could swear tears are glimmering in his eyes. "Can I still bake in the kitchens now and then? It helps me relax."

"My love, you can do anything you want." Erik gently removes me from his lap, rises, and walks over to Joseph. After kissing him, Erik presses his forehead against Joseph's and whispers something. It's not for my ears, but I can't hide a wriggle of delighted happiness at the soft display of their mutual affection.

"Through art, we will change the world's perspective on the past," Erik proclaims, stepping away from Joseph and spreading his arms as if to encompass all of us. "We will teach the truth of history through stories and promote magical tolerance through music, subtly at first, then more boldly. And one day, with our whole family working together, perhaps I will be able to step into the light as my true self, and you will all be able to reveal your magic to the world."

This, then, is the purpose of which he and Raoul spoke, the scheme for our future. Dragons and mages once again able to live freely, this time in harmony with humans.

His vision is beautiful, and so much more exciting than any career I could have dreamed for myself. I will be a part of this. All of me, body and voice, vital to the cause.

I fly to Erik impulsively, wrapping him in a hug, setting my ear against his rapidly pounding heart. Matthieu throws his arms around both of us, then reaches for Raoul and pulls him close. Joseph steps in at Erik's back and completes the knot of love.

I have never felt so completely protected, encircled, and safe. Whatever dangers lie ahead, we can face them together.

"I'm getting hard," sighs Matthieu blissfully, and Raoul laughs, an unfettered, glorious sound. The sound of freedom.

Gently extricating myself from their limbs, I strip quietly until I'm entirely naked before them. They watch in silence, and then Erik steps forward.

He throws aside his mask first. Unbuttons his waistcoat, his shirt, his pants. Sheds his socks, boots, every piece of clothing, including his underwear.

He stands opposite me, wholly naked for the first time, every muscle cut and carved to perfection, from his swelling pectorals to the tempting slanted ridges of his hips. Along the left side of his body glimmer the dark-green scales he may never be able to change. His enormous, splendid cock juts out boldly.

"Angel," I murmur. "You're beautiful."

Raoul steps to my side, undressing as well, shedding every bit of noble finery. He gives me a tearful, joyful smile, and I link my arm with his, pulling him close to my side.

Joseph shucks off his clothes slowly, while Matthieu sheds them fast and bounds naked between us, his slim cock dancing as he gives Erik a merry kiss. Then Joseph moves in, and we all slide onto the rugs together, skin slipping against skin, hard planes and soft curves.

My pussy swells with warmth, turning soft and slippery for these men, *my* men. I draw Raoul down onto the floor, and I crawl over him on my hands and knees, tucking his cock into my slick channel. He moans lightly, closing his eyes while I fuck myself on him.

Joseph approaches me silently, a dollop of lubricant in his hand. He told me about it in a whisper the night we kissed beside our wounded Matthieu. He said Erik invented the substance to soothe the passage of a cock through one's rear channel.

Joseph must carry some with him always, in case anyone needs fucking. I smirk at the thought. And then I gasp as he moves in behind me, parting my ass cheeks, circling my tiny puckered hole with the cool substance. It warms upon contact with my skin.

Joseph dips a single finger inside my asshole first, working it gently deeper, spreading the lubricant. My pussy is pulsing and warm with the rush of Raoul's cock, and I don't mind the slight discomfort. When Joseph adds a second finger to my asshole, it doesn't bother me at all.

Matthieu approaches my mouth, cupping my chin gently and tilting my face up. I open for his lovely cock, and he plunges between my lips with a sigh of relief. He leans his whole torso over my back, clasping my waist to brace himself so he can lift his ass for Erik. I'm bathed in the scent of Matthieu, of light male sweat and vanilla and a fragrance like rain-washed grass.

While I'm sucking Matthieu's cock, I have a partial view of Erik preparing a bit of lubricant, reaching into the crease of Matthieu's bottom to apply it. As Erik wedges his cock into Matthieu's hole, the blond dancer's grip on my waist tightens, and his cock jerks inside my mouth. His arousal makes me hotter and sends little dancing thrills through my entire abdomen.

Joseph is entering my rear hole now. His cock is wet with lubricant, and it slides into my ass more easily than I thought it would. The sensation of being packed full by Joseph's cock, Raoul's cock, and Matthieu's cock is such a blessed delight I can hardly bear it. My body is a riot of incredible sensations.

"I can feel Joseph's cock moving inside you, Christine," gasps Raoul. "I can feel it through the wall, surging—oh god, I'm coming, I'm coming."

"Your ass is so tight, Christine," groans Joseph. "I can't last—fuck—"

And then they are both huffing and groaning at once, spurting hot cum into both my holes. My first orgasm cracks through me, and I scream around Matthieu's cock.

"Are they both coming inside you?" he gasps. "Oh god, that is so beautiful—" and he releases with a shrill whimper, his cum flowing over my tongue, down my throat. I swallow it all and lick his pretty cock clean, giving a tiny kiss to the tip.

"Fuck, Christine," Erik says. "Could you be more adorable?"

"She really couldn't." Joseph pulls slowly out of my ass and steps back. Raoul slips out of me too and rolls aside, gasping for breath.

Trembling with fading ecstasy, I move out from beneath Matthieu. Eric supports him instead, with one muscular arm wrapped across Matthieu's chest and the other gripping his hip. I love the lines of Matthieu's slim dancer's body, his pliant submission as he is completely dominated by Erik's powerful frame. Erik pumps into him with manic urgency.

"My cock is getting hard again," Matthieu says jerkily, between thrusts. "How is that possible?"

"My influence, and the link of the nest," says Erik. "We can all have multiple orgasms if we want."

"Fuck yes," Raoul whimpers, almost crying. "Joseph, can I have your cock in my ass?"

"You want me to fuck your ass, little Vicomte?" Joseph pulls Raoul's pleasure-limp body upright and gives him a sloppy, open-mouthed kiss. I roll onto my back, propped on my elbows, and I watch their tongues entwine while I come down from my orgasm.

Erik is watching too, and he slams into Matthieu violently, roaring as he comes. Matthieu shrieks, his new erection jumping uncontrollably at the stimulation.

After Erik pulls out, he and Joseph clean their cocks. Then Joseph splays Raoul open on his back on one of the plush sofas. He rakes a hand through Raoul's auburn hair, smacks his cheek lightly while Raoul huffs a startled breath, his eyes glossy with arousal.

Roughly Joseph hauls Raoul's legs straight up, pinning them together with one burly arm. He lubricates Raoul's asshole, then noses the crown of his cock between Raoul's cheeks and toys with the puckered hole a moment before diving inside and beginning a hard, fierce rutting rhythm.

Amid the music of Raoul's cries, Erik approaches me, and I let my legs fall apart, baring my sex to him.

"Their cum is dripping out of your pretty holes, Christine," he murmurs. "So beautiful."

He trails his cock head through the liquid, rubbing it all over my pussy until I'm whining with need. Then he lifts my legs and slides into me, filling my body so beautifully I have to bite my wrist to keep from shrieking.

Matthieu sits beside me, stroking my hair while Erik fucks me. My whole body shakes as my Angel pounds harder, harder. He has already come once, so it takes longer for him to get fully erect—but he's watching my breasts bounce as he pumps into me, and I can feel his shaft heating, thickening.

Matthieu is watching my breasts too—he can't resist reaching down to fondle one of them. Erik splays a hand over my other breast, and the stimulation of the two men's fingers takes me over the edge again.

I shrill, gasp, and shake, bliss radiating sharply through my clit, pulsing upward into my belly.

"That's it, beautiful," says Matthieu. "Come for us, Christine. You belong to us. Our queen."

Erik leans down to kiss me, and as his lips touch mine, he gasps. Cum spurts into my womb, a surging, pumping heat.

"We're going to fill you with so much cum every day, Christine." Erik's breath is darkness and roses, smoke and licorice. "We're going to fuck you until you can't move."

"My turn," Matthieu moans, palming his length.

Erik drives into me one last time, a possessive thrust, and then he pulls out and yields my pussy to Matthieu. I'm relaxed and softened, completely submitted, and Matthieu lets out a shaking groan as he slides into me.

And that is only the beginning. We fuck each other almost all night, until the lair is awash with the scent of sex and wine and roses.

Before I fall asleep in a warm, comforting tangle of male limbs and bodies, I see Erik standing over his abandoned mask, stroking his cock. As he sprinkles the mask with his cum, his face wrenches in an expression like pain, then relaxes into a calm peace I've never seen on his features before.

Perhaps he was bound with tighter knots than any he used on us.

And we have finally set him free.

31

CHRISTINE

THIRTY YEARS LATER

It is opening night.

I'm singing the lead in Erik's newest opera: *L'Amour du Diable*. It's our family's love story, loosely adapted for the stage. I hope I can sustain the longest, highest notes—my belly is swelling large these days, and my breath is shorter. Erik has magically ascertained that one of the two babies sharing space in my womb belongs to him, and the other to Joseph. The two men seem intensely happy about their children growing in my belly together.

The new children will be a happy addition to the golden-haired boy and the red-haired girl who already consider the Opera House their personal playground. Matthieu and I had little Jacques first, and Charlotte is Raoul's. Right now they're in our big mansion behind the opera house, being tucked into bed by a kind, apple-cheeked woman who cares for them when the five of us are busy with a show.

Erik walks into my dressing room, nodding a greeting to the girl who does my hair and makeup. He's unmasked, his scales on full display. He can transition easily to a dragon now, but the scales along his left side are a permanent part of him, even when he's in human shape. He has learned to cast an illusion that makes the scales invisible and restores him to an entirely human appearance—but he rarely does that anymore. In this city, in this region, he is accepted and beloved, exactly as he is.

It took decades. But we did it. Erik's genius and creativity, Joseph's management, Matthieu's choreography, my voice, and Raoul's influence. Our performances became so popular that people would come from faraway regions to see them. And gradually, the subtle message of our music and stories begin to soak into the minds of our audiences. Dragons are still nearly extinct, but the few that remain are no longer hunted. In fact, there are four new dragon nests in this region.

My magic has grown. Neither the other men nor I will ever be as powerful as Erik, but I am a force to be reckoned with in my own right—a far cry from the gullible girl who arrived at L'Opera Lajeunesse so many years ago. If there was ever another Dragon War, I could defend myself and my children. And I would have three skilled mages and a dragon beside me.

Erik approaches behind me and leans over to lay a single red rose on my dressing table. Then he draws my curls aside and kisses the curve of my neck.

Behind him, Joseph, Matthieu and Raoul enter the room, all of them as young and handsome as ever, and all dressed in fine, fashionable suits selected by the Vicomte. Joseph is tugging unhappily at his tight collar. Even now, after so many years as a respected manager, he prefers loose unbuttoned shirts.

The cosmetic artist bobs a curtsy and slips out, closing the door with a secretive smile. She knows what is about to happen. The men have done this before every performance of mine, for luck.

"We're here for your pre-show orgasm, my lamb," whispers Erik against my neck. "Whose mouth or cock would you like tonight?"

I smile at them in the mirror. "I want all your mouths, one after another."

They chuckle. "As you wish," says Erik.

They lead me to the couch in the dressing room, easing me onto it, tucking a pillow at the small of my back. I sigh, placing one hand on my pregnant belly.

"We bred you well, little one," murmurs Erik, stroking my stomach. He and Joseph hold my legs apart while Raoul begins the beautiful torment of my sex. He has learned well over the past thirty years, though I privately believe Matthieu still eats pussy the best of them all.

Raoul's light beard brushes against my heavy belly and tantalizes my inner thighs. He licks me deep and slow, bathing my pussy lips all over with his tongue. A tickling warmth begins to surge inside me, liquid pooling at my core.

When Raoul rises from his knees, he wipes his damp beard and takes one of my thighs so Joseph can move in. My manager kisses my round belly first, then sinks down and begins to savor me with his broad lips and thick tongue. He licks enthusiastically, roughly, and my clit starts to pulse and thrum.

Then my Matthieu switches places with Joseph, angling his face beneath the swell of my stomach so he can tantalize my clit with his lip ring. He has more piercings now, through his nipples and at the head of his cock. His ears are lined with tiny gold hoops.

The friction of the tiny metal lip ring sends sparks through my clit, and I cry out softly, gripping Raoul's free hand. Matthieu nuzzles and laps and kisses my pussy until my thighs are shaking, quivering on the brink of orgasm.

And then my Angel of Music steps in. Kneels between my legs. Strokes my pussy with his long, quick tongue, over, and over, again, again, again— takes my clit between his lips and suckles—

The orgasm snakes through my clit, radiating through my whole pussy, along my spine. I'm coming for so long I nearly forget to breathe as wave after wave of bliss chases through my body.

"Look at her. I'm so hard," whispers Matthieu.

"You're always hard." Joseph rolls his eyes. "We don't have time to suck you off, Matt. There's a show starting soon. You must oversee the dancers."

"Fuck me later?" Matthieu grins at him brightly.

"We should all fuck you later," Raoul speaks up. "It's been a while since we did a themed night. Our theme this evening can be 'Matthieu's tight man-pussy.'"

"Oh, I like that." Matthieu's lashes drift shut. "Oh god—I'm coming in my pants. *Merde*, I really am coming in my pants—fuck, ahhh—"

Joseph reaches for Matthieu's crotch, then lifts wet fingers. "Damn you, you actually did, you little slut," he growls. "Your cum soaked right through. Go and change quickly."

Matthieu glances at me, half-panting, half-laughing, and I can't help grinning back at him. Joseph smacks his ass as he runs out.

Erik is still tenderly licking me, cleaning all my juices. Then he and Raoul dry my pussy and help me step into fresh panties.

The care they give to me, always—it fills my heart so full I want to cry. But I don't, because then my poor cosmetic artist will have to repaint my lashes and lids.

"We will be applauding you from Box 5." Erik bends slightly and kisses my lips. Then he takes my jaw in his hand. "No naughty gestures this time. The crowd may not notice your rebellion, but I do. I see everything, remember? Disobey me, and I will have to bind you. You may be pregnant, but I can still tie your arms and legs together with such beautiful knots. I will leave you immobile on the bed, unable to touch yourself while the boys and I perform all manner of debauchery in your presence."

"Promise?" I whisper.

He snarls faintly and kisses me again, his dragon's canine grazing my lip.

When he moves away, Raoul kisses me as well. "Drink plenty of water," he advises. "If you feel faint, signal to one of the stagehands, or to the prop master. I've told the other performers to catch you if you faint."

"Raoul." I cup his face in my hands. "I will be fine. Stop worrying."

With an apologetic smile, he follows Erik to the door. Joseph kisses me too, with one hand clasping my nape, a possessive gesture. The heat in his eyes says everything—his love and his concern for me, the anxiety he suffers on every opening night.

I press my hand over his heart and whisper. "I love you."

"I love you, too, succubus." He kisses me again.

Then he and Raoul leave.

Erik stays while I finish getting ready, and then he walks me through the hall until we reach the backstage area. There is a silent, frantic hustle going on as the remaining set pieces are moved into place, as the chorus takes their final sips of water and the ballet dancers chalk their shoes. The overture is in full swing, approaching the moment when the curtain will rise on Act One.

Erik's hand rests against my lower back. "I will be listening to my music soaring from your throat, my little lamb."

"I hope I please you, Angel," I whisper.

"Of course you will, sweetheart." He smiles, backing away, receding into the shadows. "You always do."

I move onto the stage and find my mark. There's an excited stir in my belly—the babies kicking because they can hear the music. It makes me smile.

The curtain rises, the lights flare, and in their glow, I begin to sing.

Jessamine Rue is a pen name.
I have written many books,
But this is my first reverse harem.
If this book succeeds,
And people enjoy it,
I may write another one like it.
We shall see.
Please rate and review.

Made in United States
Cleveland, OH
12 March 2025

15090876R00164